MW01118197

HAPPILY EVER AFTER

HAPPILY EVER AFTER

MELANIE MARTINS

Melanie Martins

BOOK FOUR

BLOSSOM IN WINTER V

Melanie Martins, LLC
melaniemartins.com

First published in the United States by Melanie Martins, LLC in 2021.

ISBSN ebook 979-8-9852380-7-5

ISBN Paperback 979-8-9852380-3-7

Printed and bound by CPI Group (UK) Ltd, Croydon, CR0 4YY

This is a 1st Edition.

DISCLAIMER

This novel is a work of fiction written in American English and is intended for mature audiences. Names, characters, places, and incidents are either the product of the author's imagination or are used fictitiously. Any resemblance to actual persons, living or dead, is entirely coincidental. This novel contains strong and explicit language, graphic sexuality, and other sensitive content that may be disturbing for some readers.

To all of you, my dear readers.
Thank you.

CHAPTER 1

Manhattan, January 31, 2022
Petra

"You aren't supposed to have your phone on until the plane lands," I hiss.

Emma just rolls her eyes as she continues typing. "It's a jet. We can have our phones on." She then looks out the window and adds, "Plus, the plane hasn't started its descent yet, so it's fine."

Truthfully, all I want is for Emma to stop checking her phone every two minutes in the hopes that she'll receive an apology from Yara—I know that's what she's longing for.

We haven't spoken much since the plane took off. Emma's spent most of her time either listening to music or sleeping and doesn't seem too willing to open up. I know she needs time alone to heal, but that also means she needs to stay away from Yara—and not just in the physical sense.

"Emma, Yara doesn't love you," I remind her once more. "She just wants to control you like a toy." Before Emma can step in and take offense, I decide to disclose what I found out about my sister-in-law in the hopes it'll help her to move on. "She never stopped having sex with Elliot, by the way. What she told you was a lie."

Her mouth gapes in shock and her eyes remain fixed on me like she just froze at the news.

It hurts me to see her like that, but this is something she needed to hear.

"How would you know that?" she finally asks.

"I found an archived article about her and Elliot leaving a fertility clinic, dating back not even a year ago."

"Fuck," she blurts out, her eyes drifting down to her lap as she processes everything. "Why are you telling me this now?"

"I just found out when we were in St. Moritz," I tell her. "And I didn't want to tell you while Yara was around."

She nods, clearly considering me before asking, "You were scared I'd confront Yara about it and tell her it was you, huh?"

I exhale a bit slower, pondering her question. "Yeah, God knows what she's capable of. I'd rather not piss her off any more than I have."

The jet is finally circling Teterboro, and I'm more than ready to be home. The trip to St. Moritz had only been a few days long, but it felt closer to weeks that I'd been away from my husband and children. Not to mention the insane tension I'd endured our last day there. New York, previously the center of all the drama in my life, was starting to look like a calm and peaceful paradise.

Emma's phone pings, and I watch her face carefully. Her expression is soft, but there's a line of worry between her perfectly arched brows. "What's up?" I ask.

"Just look," she says, handing the phone over to me.

Fortunately, it's a message from Shiori, who Emma had in her phone simply as "Shi" followed by a black heart emoji.

I really enjoyed seeing you in St. Moritz. I'm about to fly to Tokyo. The exhibition starts this Sunday. If you want to come, I'll have a plane waiting for you on Friday, at 10 AM. No pressure.

I can't help the smile that pulls at the corner of my mouth. Shiori had been the perfect candidate to drag Emma away from Yara, but I hadn't expected to like her so much as a person too. Thoughts of couples' trips with Shiori and Emma and Alex and I, flit through my mind. It's such a departure from Emma chasing Yara across the globe for a scrap of her attention.

But I try to hide my emotions, as I don't want Emma thinking that I'm pressuring her one way or the other. She has to be free to make her own choices; all I can do is gently nudge her in the right direction.

"So," I start, "are you going to go or not?"

Emma sinks into the leather plane seat, groaning as she scrubs her hands over her face. "I don't know yet. I want to, but I know if I do, it'll be the last nail in the coffin for Yara and me. You know I love her despite everything."

"I know you do," I respond gently. "But that's a dead-end road, and we both know it."

11

"I've got a few days to think about it," she hedges, taking her phone back when I offer it to her and pocketing it.

"Just don't base your decision off of any loyalty you have for Yara or fear of hurting her. Remember that she's still with her husband, so it's not like she's being loyal to you."

"Obviously," she snaps, but there is sadness in her voice. "I didn't forget she's still a married woman, and I know perfectly well she isn't gonna divorce him anytime soon. I'm just…" she lets her words trail off as she thinks something through. "I thought I could play without getting myself burned, but I was wrong. And now I'm fucked."

Despite her language, I don't take offense at her attitude. I know that she's hurting, and I don't want to make her feel any worse. I'm just desperate for her to make the decision that will make her happy in the long run. "I won't push anymore," I tell her, reclining back in my seat. "We can drop it for now."

She sighs before nodding. "Yes, please, I want to talk about something other than my love life, for once."

We talk about anything else we can as the plane descends; what Emma plans on doing when she isn't torn between two women, my schoolwork, the twins, and the gallery. I've been considering hiring a teacher for a children's art class in the gallery, so parents could browse and enjoy all the artwork while their kids learned for an hour or two. It's something the twins could enjoy as they got older, too.

We're discussing what portion of the gallery would be best suited to be changed into a classroom when we finally touch down at Teterboro. I've never been so excited about returning home from a vacation than I am currently. We could've been at literally the closest thing to heaven on earth, and it still wouldn't have felt right without my family.

Looking out of the window, I notice there are two sleek, black cars waiting for us as the plane taxis around. My heart jumps in excitement as I find Alex leaning against one car with his arms full of flowers. The day is overcast, cold, and dreary, but seeing him is like looking upon the sun itself. Jeez, I'm so happy to be back in New York!

When the front door is finally open and we receive the okay to go, I come running out of the plane while Alex sits the bouquet on top of the car, catching me in his arms as I come flying down the stairs. He grabs me around the waist and spins me, and it seems as if all the tension flows away like water in his arms. It's only been a few days, but it was still too long.

"Did you have a good time?" he asks into my hair, kissing the top of the head.

"Not really," I whisper back, not wanting Emma to hear. Alex laughs and sits me back on my feet before pressing a chaste kiss on my lips. I hum in approval, leaning into him, but he separates earlier than I'd prefer.

"Later," he promises. "Right now, let's get you out of the cold and back home."

"Emma?" I call over to her, where she's directing her driver to load her luggage into her ride. "Are you okay if I go, or do you want me to wait with you?"

She waves her hand dismissively. "You're fine. I'm sure you're dying to get back to your wife life."

I wrinkle my nose, and she laughs. I'm glad to see her looking more relaxed. St. Moritz had gotten her closer than ever to Shiori, but it'd also been a tense and fraught few days.

"Call me later," I demand, hustling over to hug her close before leaving. "I know you'll make the right decision, Em. You know I just want what's best for you."

"Me and my self-destructive tendencies," she says, giving me a last squeeze before pushing me back toward my husband. "I'll talk to you later."

This time, I let Alex hand me the flowers instead of immediately jumping on him. It's a sunny mix of roses and wildflowers that makes me think of spring and how much I miss the warmth and greenery. Despite loving winter, I feel like I've had enough snow to last me a lifetime. I lower my face into the arrangement until the petals tickle my nose and inhale deeply.

"I love them," I assure Alex, kissing his stubbled cheek.

He opens the car door for me, and I climb into the back. Alex usually drives us himself whenever he can, but this time he's brought a driver. Smart move, considering I wanted all his attention on me and nowhere else.

He slides in beside me, and I immediately scoot to the middle seat, setting my bouquet carefully in the vacant seat. The inside of the car is warm and smells like peppermint and Alex's cologne, and I exhale hugely in relief. He raises his arm over the headrest of the seat, and I immediately snuggle up next to him, resting my head on his shoulder.

When the car starts driving us away, Alex pulls me close to him and we sit in silence for a while, just soaking in each other's company. It'd only been a short time apart, but it was sweet to realize he missed me just as much as I had missed him.

"So, was it really all that bad?" he asks finally.

"Well, let's see. Where do I start?" I inhale, pondering my next set of words. "It was cold like everywhere else I've been lately, Emma was on edge, your sister was planning my untimely death the entire time, and I had to be in the middle of a love triangle between my best friend, an artist I'm working with, and my sister-in-law." I blow out an exhausted breath. "It wasn't really a great time, but it was absolutely *gorgeous*. I'd love to go back the four of us."

"We can probably arrange that," he agrees. "In the off-season, it's particularly peaceful. And not quite as cold."

"Sounds perfect," I answer.

"How did your secret mission go, though?" he half-jokes. "Did you manage to get your wayward friend set up with the world-famous artist?"

"I'd say we're about eighty percent there, give or take," I tell him honestly. "Yara has her claws into Emma deep, but since Shiori is letting Emma come to her and not the other way around, Emma should be able to break away on her own."

Alex chuckles. "I'm sure my sister was apoplectic."

I think about how close Yara had come to physical violence when I had met with her alone at her villa, and cringe. "I don't know what the obsession is with her. Yara is married, has kids, money, a family, and a high-profile polo career. Why does she hang onto Emma so tightly?"

"Honestly? I think Emma cracked something open in my sister's frozen heart." Alex's tone is only half-amused. "All of us siblings have a hard time admitting what we really want, especially if it doesn't follow the exact path Mother sat out for us." He rests his chin on my hair, and I'm sure he must be thinking about how hard it had been for him and me to come together.

"I wish I'd known I'd be playing relationship therapist for so many people once you and I got married."

"Hopefully it's only a onetime thing," he says, before looking me in the eye again. "Speaking of my family, though... Did anyone call you while you were in St. Moritz?"

I consider lying to Alex about his mom's call. As of right now, if Emma flew out to meet Shiori in Japan, I was free and clear of Margaret's drama, and we could live in peace. But I wouldn't want Alex to lie to me in the same situation, so I tell him the truth. "Your mom called, actually."

I explain the phone call to him, and when he seems worried that the Yara and Emma thing might not be completely settled, I assure him that we are on the right track. The sooner I can get Margaret off our shoulders, the better. Alex still seems pensive after that, looking down at me a few times as if he wants to speak before turning away. He sighs heavily, and I worry that something is going unsaid.

"Love," I say, sitting up so I can look him in the eye. "Is everything okay? You're acting fidgety. Do you want to talk about something?"

He takes a second to answer, but shakes his head, giving an unconvincing grin before kissing me gently. "I just missed you, that's all," he says when he pulls back. I purse my lips, searching his face, but he doesn't budge. Fine. He'd come clean soon enough, whatever it is.

But it doesn't matter for now, anyway. We are minutes away from home, and I'm almost vibrating with excitement about seeing the kids. I schooled myself on the plane to not be too over the top when I get my hands on them again. I don't want to scare them, or for them to pick up on my emotions and become upset too. The unfortunate fact is that there would be times we'd have to be apart over the years, hopefully never for long, but they and I both have to learn to live with the absences and only take joy in coming home.

"We'll have lunch at home with the kids, just the four of us," he informs me, as if he can sense how excited I am to see them again.

There is a list as long as my arms of things I need to do now that I'm back in Manhattan, including schoolwork and everything with the gallery, but there's only one thing on my agenda today, and that is to kiss my babies.

* * *

Thankfully, Alex doesn't try to drag me into any more conversations that would require my full attention, because I wouldn't be able to focus, anyway. Once we pull up to the curb, I realize I'm just a few minutes away from my kids, and I mentally force myself to stay calm.

I step out of the car and wait for Alex before making my way inside the building. I'd been having a touch of anxiety about this moment if I was being honest with myself. Were the twins old enough to realize that I had left? And if so, had it hurt their feelings for me to leave them here? Not that they could understand why I had left, but certainly they had noticed I was gone.

I shouldn't have worried though. When I crack the door to the condo open, trying to be quiet in case the twins are down for a nap, I see Lily is sitting with them in the living room, reading them a children's book while they watch her raptly, eyes and mouths open wide. If there had ever been someone made for a job with children, it was Lily.

Everyone turns to me, and the change in the babies is immediate. They are all gummy smiles and giggles as I hustle over to kneel down with them, sweeping both of their chubby bodies into my arms for a squeeze.

I'd get better at being apart from them. I had to, with the life we lived, but for now, I was going to bask in this moment. No one was going to tell me my reactions were over the top.

Jasmine and Jasper are warm and soft, their hair smelling of the lavender baby shampoo they love so much. They babble to me as I kiss their round cheeks, almost as if they are telling me a story, while busy hands pull at my collar and hair, and I love every second of it.

"Have they behaved?" I ask Lily, spitting out a chunk of my hair where Jasmine had dragged it over my mouth.

"Oh no, they've been terrible," Lily teases, shutting the children's book and standing. "They were perfect as always, Petra. Did you enjoy yourself?"

"No. Yes. It's a long story," I blurt out amid a quick laugh.

"At least the family is reunited," she says cheerily. "I'll leave you four to your lunch now that you're home. Call me if you need me."

I want to spend some more time with the twins before we sit down to eat, and after shrugging off his winter coat, Alex joins me. Both Jasmine and Jasper have been getting stronger every day, and it's a joy to watch them thrive. Jasmine is still behind Jasper in weight and physical milestones, but mentally she's proved time and time again that she's just as capable as her brother.

Jasper raises himself to his hands and knees and rocks back and forth, eventually showing us his shaky crawling talents, to which Alex and I both cheer and clap—much to his delight. His sister is not one to be shown up, and while she can't support herself fully on her hands and knees yet, she drags herself in an army crawl across the carpet, huffing with the effort. Of course, we congratulate her just as much, and by the time they're finished, we're all laughing. It's good to be home.

Lunch isn't over the top, thankfully. I'm a bit burnt out on the extravagant food from the polo tournament, and the chickpea salad Maria has whipped up for us is perfectly light and refreshing. Alex and I have become pros at feeding the twins in tandem with ourselves now, and our conversation flows naturally as we enjoy our meal together.

Except... I can still see some sort of apprehension on Alex's face. I'm sure something must've happened while I was gone that he doesn't want to share, but I can't imagine what it can be. I highly doubt his mom has been bothering him—

considering how satisfied she had sounded on the phone with me—but she's the only member of Alex's family, aside from Yara, that I can imagine actively trying to cause any sort of chaos in our lives. I decide to go off that hunch and see how he reacts.

"Your mother was very brusque when I talked to her," I comment between bites. "Did she say anything else to you, or are we done with her for the time being?"

Alex shakes his head, the wariness on his face growing. "I haven't spoken to her since you left."

"Oh." I push my salad around my plate as I think of a new approach. "None of your other sisters were at Yara's polo tournament, which surprised me a little. When's the last time you heard from them?"

Alex sets his fork down with a sigh and rubs one hand over his face. Jasmine squawks in protest, and he quickly feeds her another bite of her sweet potato puree while he collects his thoughts.

"Did Julia call you?" Alex asks simply.

I raise my eyebrows, genuinely surprised. Is every member of the Van Dieren family going to poke their fingers into my day-to-day life this year? It's only January!

"Definitely not," I respond. "I haven't spoken to her since the the twins' baptism. You know that. Why would she call me?"

A few moments of silence goes by before he finally says, "She called me, but I got the impression it was you she wanted to speak to."

"Wow." I take a long sip of my water, contemplating what all this could mean. "After everything she did to me—to us

—she's still trying to be in your life?" I can't keep the indignation out of my tone.

Alex grimaces. "It's weird, yeah…."

I know my husband well enough to see that he isn't telling me the entire story. "You seem worried," I comment gently, trying to let him know that this wasn't an interrogation. "Did she tell you something in particular?"

He takes a sip of his water, his posture stiffer than usual. "She just wanted to fill me in about some news going on in their lives. The conversation kind of fizzled out when she figured out you weren't around to talk."

I shoot him an arched eyebrow. "Is something wrong with her or her family?" As much as the Van Dieren clan grated on my last nerves, I'd never wish ill on any of them— especially not his nieces and nephews.

"They're all fine, from what I can tell."

Alex's mouth is tight, and he ignores his meal now, focusing solely on our daughter, who obediently opens her mouth like a baby bird for each bite he gives her. I watch him closely while I feed Jasper until my spoon scrapes the bottom of his bowl. Full of sweet potatoes, his eyes are droopy, and he yawns hugely.

"Maria?" I call out. "Can you and Lily take the twins up for a nap?"

"Yes, ma'am!" Maria pipes up from the other room, and I hear her talking to Lily through the intercom in her basement apartment.

Alex must know that I'm about to grill him for information, because my no-nonsense, scared of nothing husband looks decidedly uncomfortable. I wipe the twins' faces and give them quick kisses before Lily arrives to sweep them off for a midday nap, and then Alex and I are alone.

This conversation would probably be better held in the living room or somewhere more comfortable, but I don't want to wait. Most of all, I want to wipe that worried expression from his handsome face. I stand and saunter over to my husband, and he looks surprised when I lower myself into his lap, wrapping my arms around his neck.

"What's wrong, Alex?" I ask in a whisper, leaning forward so my forehead rests against his. He sighs deeply, running his hands up and down my back. "You can trust me."

"It's just…" he lets his words trail off, clearly thinking something through. "It's such a shame they did what they did to us."

It's a vague statement, but it's at least something. "She's trying to reconnect with you, huh?"

"Yeah," he blurts out, an exasperated breath rolling off his mouth. "I know she doesn't deserve it. But I was very close to my sisters, especially Julia and Sebastian, so it's hard to simply forget they exist."

I think of Alex as a much younger man, laughing with his siblings, all of them light and free from the shackles their lives would force upon them. Since I was raised as an only child, I can't imagine how hard it must be for him to let all of those relationships fade away as all the scheming and underhanded plans have replaced the simple love between brothers and sisters. It isn't fair for Alex… but on the other hand; I'm not comfortable with putting myself right back into the snake pit with his siblings for the sake of it.

"Do you miss them?" I ask gently, already knowing the answer. He needs to say it out loud, though; he needs to vent before it destroys him inside.

"Sometimes," he confesses, his voice low. "It's Sebastian's fifty-fifth birthday in about three weeks, and I know she wanted me to be present, but I declined her invitation." His grip on me tightens, and I let him bury his face in my neck, breathing deeply. "I hate this, Petra. What they did to us, how hard it has been on you… I wish I could fix it for us all. Jasmine and Jasper make me realize every single day how much I wish I could watch my nieces and nephews grow up."

"You did well," I tell him, tilting his face to mine with a finger under his chin. His ocean-blue eyes are tired, the lines at the corners of them strained. I kiss those corners, and then the sloping bones of his cheeks and jaw, and finally his mouth. "It might not have been easy, but it was the right choice for where we are right now. Things can change in the future *maybe*, but you did the right thing for our family right now. Thank you, Alex."

He kisses me back, his lips soft and warm. "It's so good to hear you say that. Until now, I was still full of doubts on whether I had made the right call." He hesitates, as if reluctant to ask the next question. "Petra? Would you be…" he stops mid-sentence, as if hesitating whether or not to say the rest. His eyes drift up to meet mine, and amid the silence, I give a quick nod for him to go ahead. "Open to repairing these relationships, as long as they worked to make it up to us?"

"Alex!" I snap, totally taken aback by his question. Should I tell him no? Of course I should! And a part of me wants to, but it feels harder than I thought, so I try to come up with a more diplomatic and mature answer, an answer that wouldn't hurt either of us. "I'd never deny you your family, even if it's hard for me," I find myself saying. "The time in Aspen with your mom should prove that to you. As long as it doesn't hurt our marriage or our children, then I guess I'm open to it. But you have to promise me you'll put the twins and me first." It sounds vague enough, open but not too much.

"Always," he says in a low voice.

"And you have to realize that I won't simply forgive and forget. As far as I'm concerned, they're all in the wrong, and don't deserve any empathy from me."

Alex chuckles. "I wouldn't expect anything else from you, my stubborn wife."

I can feel the relief in his body at having it all out in the open. I knew now that Julia wanted something from me, but neither Alex nor I know what exactly. I'll have to talk to her sometime this week. I'm relieved he didn't give her my new number, as I don't know what I would have done having to deal with one more sister in St. Moritz. Back on my home turf, I feel more confident in facing her.

"Now that that's settled…" I brush my nose along the side of his. "I could really use a shower, and maybe someone to wash my back for me."

"Is that an invitation?" Alex rumbles, nipping at my jaw.

"It could be," I tease. "Maybe more of a request." I need to wash away the stress of the weekend and all the drama that came with it. What better place to start than reminding my husband just why he missed me so much?

"Invite accepted." Alex stands quickly, and I squeal as he shifts me into a fireman carry over his shoulder before I dissolve into helpless giggles. With a hand planted firmly on my backside, he carries me up the stairs and into our bedroom.

He drops me on our bed and helps me strip out of my clothes, and I do the same for him, scooting to the edge of the mattress and pulling him forward by the waistband of his pants. He lets me undo the button and zipper, pushing them down his legs, and I can tell he's happy to have me home. I run my fingers along the band of his briefs and look up at him, a mischievous grin on my face.

"Did you miss me?"

He takes one of my hands and lays it over the bulge of his erection, raising one eyebrow. "What do you think?"

I know I told him I wanted to go for a shower, but right now, all I do is tug his briefs down and watch as his manhood pops out, hard and ready for me. He hisses when I wrap a hand around him and stroke. Heat starts rolling off of his body as he threads his fingers in my hair and draws my face forward until my lips brush the tip of him. I snake my tongue out and drag it over the tip, and I feel his whole body shudder.

"Fuck…" he rasps, pulling me in further. I oblige, every little noise and sigh he makes feeding my need for him.

I take his cock as deep as I can into my mouth until he is bumping the back of my throat before pulling me away again. With my hands free, I run them over the taut muscles of his legs and thighs, never able to get enough even as I'm swallowing him.

I hum against his skin and his grip in my hair gets tighter, right on that delicious edge of pain and pleasure. I want him to finish like this, but I know he isn't going to allow it, and when I circle my tongue around the head each time he pulls back, I know he's reaching the end of his rope.

Finally, he pulls me completely away, his hand moving from my scalp to cup my jaw, chest heaving as if he had run a marathon.

"Shower. Now," he demands.

I shed the last of my clothes as I stumble behind him to the bathroom, where he has turned on the shower and steam is already filling the room. The heat of it feels wonderful on my skin after the chill of the bedroom and I sigh as Alex, now fully nude, takes my hand and pulls me beneath the falling water.

The marble shower with the rainfall showerhead makes it almost seem like another world when Alex closes the glass door, shutting us away from reality. I immediately lean into his body, and he lets me, sliding his hands up and down my back to my butt. Between his touch and the water, I shiver from the sensations, feeling at once both content and needy.

After a few moments, his wandering hands make their way between my legs, one hand wrapping my leg around his waist while the other parts my folds, one of his fingers pushing deep to test my readiness. He must like what he finds because he pulls out and pushes two fingers in next. The feeling of him stretching me is intoxicating, and all the nerves in my body seem to come alive.

"Lean against the wall," he says, voice raspy.

I let myself lean backward until my back is flush to the cold marble, one leg still wrapped around Alex's waist. He slowly pulls his fingers out of me and grasps his cock in his hand, guiding himself to my entrance.

"We'll go slower later," he tells me through clenched teeth. "But right now, I've got to have you."

All I can muster is a thready, "Please."

He doesn't leave me waiting, thrusting deep, and it's so sudden I almost feel like my body is protesting the invasion. Having him fill me up so suddenly teeters right on the edge of being too much, but he stays still long enough for me to adjust before repeating the movement again. This time, it's nothing but pleasure.

His eyes search my face for any lingering signs of distress, and when he finds none, he fucks me in earnest, the movements of his body sharp and steady, meant to bring us both to the edge. No teasing or drawn-out seductions today. Just his body, mine, and the falling cascade of water we stand beneath.

I try to brace myself on the wall, but when I continue to slide, I give up and put all my trust in Alex, holding onto him as he continues to piston into me, the sound of our flesh slapping together echoing in the stone room. It's all I can do to keep my own cries quieted to just whimpers.

As we make our way to the peak of our climaxes together, he captures my mouth in a searing kiss, giving me no mercy as he nips my bottom lip with his teeth before his tongue explores me. With the onslaught of his cock moving in and out of me, and our mouths locked together, I feel like I've lost myself in him. Like I don't know where I end, and he begins.

We reach a shuddering orgasm within seconds of each other, and I'm thankful for his hand cupping the back of my head before I can throw it back on the hard marble. He's basically holding all of my weight at this point, while pleasure courses over every inch of me, even as I feel his hips still against me while he comes.

Eventually, though, even Alex's strength starts to wane. "You're going to have to stand, love," he whispers, brushing my slicked back hair from my shoulder.

"Fine," I groan, lowering my shaking leg from around his waist onto the tile floor. His cum is running down my thighs, somehow hotter than the shower water. I still don't feel steady, but I couldn't expect him to hold me forever.

We wash each other with languid strokes, and I shiver with pleasure as Alex shampoos my hair for me, his fingertips strong on my scalp. I return the favor by rubbing his tense shoulders when I wash his back, peppering kisses on his neck and shoulder blades as I do so.

"I love you," I say simply once we are done, relaxing and wasting a copious amount of water, I'm sure.

"I'd hope so, at this point," he quips. "I have a little work to do, wife, once we're done here. I hate leaving when you just got home, but—"

"I understand," I assure him. "I've got to get organized for the week anyway and with this much distraction..." I run my hands over his sculpted chest. "I won't get anything done."

He tweaks one of my nipples in response and I yelp before he thumbs it soothingly, repeating the action with my other nipple once he's finished.

Heat spreads from my chest to my core, and before I know it, we're making out again, my hands clenched on his firm arms while he kisses me.

"No." Alex pulls back suddenly, but my sadness is cooled when he laughs sardonically. "You're too tempting, you little siren. Let's get out of here before I have you up against this wall again."

I pout but end up laughing too as he pulls me out of the shower with his hand in mine. He immediately wraps me in a huge fluffy towel as if it was almost painful for him to look at me naked anymore.

After we dress, Alex kisses me once more, chastely this time, I notice with amusement. We both dress, stealing little caresses as I brush my wet hair out and apply lotion on my skin.

Just as I'm pulling on my jeans after Alex walks out the bedroom door, the baby monitor crackles, and when I turn to look at the screen, both twins have woken up, Jasper blearily staring at his mobile while Jasmine stretches hugely.

I wonder if Maria or Lily are around, but I don't see anyone as I walk out of the bedroom and make my way down to the nursery.

* * *

My workload for the day is bigger than I thought, and after getting Jasmine and Jasper up from their naps, changed, and giving them a snack, I'm now hours behind the schedule I had planned for today. Mostly because of my interlude with Alex, but that was neither here nor there.

Luckily, nothing is pressing, and I have no deadlines for today, but I really need to get everything lined up for the upcoming week. So reluctantly, I turn the babies back over to Lily when she arrives and head up to my makeshift office.

It isn't an office, really, but a corner of the atelier I had set aside for studying and when I needed to work on my laptop without being disturbed by the hustle and bustle of the house. Here it's quieter, and I'm surrounded by my own artwork, making it my special little space in the condo. String lights and pictures of my friends and family, along with a few small pots of succulents complete the cozy picture.

Being winter, the sun set early today, and I'm just packing my things back into my backpack when my phone pings on the desk. Curious to who would be messaging me, I stop what I'm doing to check it right away.

It's from Emma, which surprises me. I thought she'd need some time away from her phone and social media to decompress after St. Moritz, considering how she and Shiori's pictures were plastered over every feed and gossip rag. I cringe internally, knowing how it feels to have your romantic affairs out for all the world to see. It isn't pleasant, to say the least.

I lower myself back into my chair and open the message. It's a picture of three different paintings—the first one is uncomfortably familiar; the second one I'd only seen once before; and the last one is brand new and I'm immediately jealous of my friend for now owning it. Nevertheless, it's a very interesting picture displaying two portraits of Shiori, and one of Yara in the middle.

The first portrait I recognize is, of course, the nude piece I painted for my sister-in-law. It's, by far, the most uncomfortable thing I've ever done, and it made me feel even worse when I found out who received it. Yara is stunning, no doubt, with the lines of her muscular body arched and on display, but it's also garish, just like the woman herself. In my opinion, it feels like a piece to remind Emma of how superior Yara thought herself to be, and how grateful Emma should feel.

Next is the portrait Emma bought from the auction and agreed to display at my gallery for a period of time. As I come to think of it, I'm more than thrilled to be able to display a portrait of such a world-famous artist. Shi's portrait is calculated, serious, and represents the secretive woman that only showed a carefully crafted image of herself to the public. The third portrait that Emma received, though, is something different. Not as polished, but more intimate—vulnerable, even.

The canvas is similarly sized, but it isn't filled to every corner with color like Yara's. It's of Shiori, from the shoulders up, laying in what appears to be soft green grass scattered with cherry blossom petals. Shi's face is turned away, looking slightly to the side as if she's looking at a lover lying next to her. One delicate hand is positioned in the grass above her head, and the portrait is so detailed I can see the flecks of paint on her fingers.

The portrait is quiet, gentle, and it fades out at the edges as if in a dream. Unlike the digital paintings Shiori is so famous for, this one is done in oils, one of my preferred mediums, meaning Shiori painted this painstakingly for Emma. I hadn't heard of Shi doing traditional art in *years*. I knew in my bones that this portrait would never be in my gallery—It was something secret for Emma, something crafted for her from the heart.

Jeez, I spent so much time combing over Shi's portrait that I almost forgot to read Emma's message.

Why do I have to choose between the two? Why can't I have both?

It's simple, but I can sense the pain in it, nonetheless. I flip back and forth between the portraits again; one a trophy, the other a gift from a lover, before responding.

Because one is liberating you while the other is destroying you.

CHAPTER 2

My first morning back at home is perfectly normal and domestic, just how I like it. The only downside is not getting to stay home after breakfast. I can usually get away with doing my homework on my laptop with the twins in their bouncers or playpens next to me—or even on a huge blanket spread out on the floor so they can roll and crawl around to their heart's content—but today I have to conduct a few interviews for a personal assistant position to help me handle the gallery's workload while I'm going to school full time. A PA would also be the perfect buffer to give me space to focus on my studies while also helping me to make the right professional decisions when it comes to the gallery.

So, after breakfast, I wiggle myself into a comfortable pair of black jeans and a dusky rose blouse and grab the folder of resumes that Alex had set out for me before leaving. He's so organized that it makes me a touch envious. I hope I can get to that point one day.

After a bunch of kisses, I leave the twins with Lily. In the car's backseat, I switch on the heated leather seat and leaf through the stack of papers, thinking about what I really wanted out of a personal assistant. Someone to take all the calls and make all the appointments for all of my meetings with artists, dealers, and press so I can focus on school is a must, but I also want someone that can act as my stand-in when I'm not able to be there in person. I want to be as hands on as possible, but I don't want to wear myself thin if I can't help it.

My PA will also have to be someone that understands I'm in the public eye quite a bit and that there might be times the media becomes pushy with everyone in my social circle. So whoever I hire will have to have a good backbone for those sorts of things, and be someone who doesn't frighten easily.

"We're here," Zach informs me politely, and I realize he had pulled up to the curb a few minutes ago while I had been lost in thought.

"Sorry!" I chirp, grabbing my things and buttoning my coat.

"Do you want me to park and wait on you to finish, ma'am?"

"That's unnecessary, Zach, but thank you. I'll call you when I'm ready."

He turns to look at me, apprehension on his face, but he doesn't argue. "If you're sure. I'll see you later this afternoon."

Emma, being in the public eye so much, must have Alex's people on edge, but I have been nothing but a background character in all that. The tabloids that ran news about Shiori and Emma were, for the most part, using pictures of the two of them alone. Only a few featured me standing awkwardly in the background.

The gallery is closed to the public today while I hold my interviews, so there's no one inside except for Tilly—the gallery supervisor—who's talking with a few people in professional attire. They must be some of my candidates. I square my shoulders and give everyone a polite smile.

"Good morning, Petra," Tilly says, nodding her head at me. "When shall I send up your first candidate?"

I give a quick wave to the interviewees. "Give me ten minutes to get settled in."

Tilly walks with me as I head up the grand staircase to the upstairs offices, her hands clasped behind her back as she talks. "I wanted to inform you I had a call early this morning from Columbia's newspaper asking to take some pictures of the gallery for a piece they're doing. I told them we were closed to the public today, but they'd still like to stop in if you're alright with it."

I mull the idea over, but knowing that these journalists are studying at the same university as me makes me feel more at ease about letting them in.

"As long as they aren't underfoot and don't overstay their welcome, that's fine with me."

"Wonderful. I'll give them a call back."

Now that we're out of earshot of the PA candidates, I pause at the top of the stairs and ask, "Do you have any early impressions of them?"

Tilly purses her lips in thought. "I have an idea of which one would be *my* pick, but I don't want to put my bias on your decision, so how about I give you my opinion once you're done interviewing them?"

"That's fair," I say with a smile. "You can send the first one up in a few minutes."

I watch Tilly descend to the first floor again, her tall, rail-thin frame, dressed in her trademark black, looking perfectly at ease and in control of the gallery. She's been such a perfect fit that I was afraid none of the personal assistant candidates would stack up. The PA that Alex had lent me did an admirable job of keeping everything organized, but like all Alex's employees, he has absolutely no understanding of the current art market. In contrast, all of my candidates have some experience with the art world—from a previous contemporary art teacher to an art business major that had just graduated. But being educated in art is only half the battle. I need a middle ground between Alex's PA and my own.

While my home office is cozy and a bit fantastical with its fairy lights and hand-painted flowerpots, my office at the gallery had been coming together to look professional yet artistic with plenty of personal touches to make it feel like my very own. After looking over the schedule for the interviews and arranging the resumes in the correct order, all I have to do is wait for the first candidate to come in.

* * *

At first, it feels strange interviewing people much older than I am and I have to reference the sheet of questions Alex included for me a few times, but after a while, I fall into a rhythm. There are four people I'm scheduled to speak with today, and two tomorrow. If no one turns out to be a good fit, we'd have to set up another round of interviews, but I'm confident I'll find the right person.

The first two candidates are young women. The former art teacher is first and then an art major with a minor in management is second. Both are very qualified, polite, and seem capable, but the first woman seemed too gentle and her overly cheerful nature from teaching seemed to bleed over in how she spoke to me. I don't think she meant to be, but her tone felt condescending in a way I didn't love.

Candidate number two was more serious, but she seemed fixated on the gallery itself and not on the work I would need her to do as my personal assistant. Still, it might just have been her trying to connect with me on a personal level over our shared interests in art, so I wasn't ruling her out completely. She's clearly incredibly knowledgeable, so that's a big plus.

The third candidate is a young man, taller than me but shorter than my husband. He's dressed in a Tiffany blue button-up and charcoal gray slacks, every ounce of his outfit is perfectly tailored, with an impeccably clean haircut and thin-rimmed glasses perched on his nose to round it all off. He introduces himself as Mason Palmer with a quick handshake before settling in the taupe chair across the desk from me. I can't help but notice the thin, black wedding band he's wearing, which complements his deeply tanned complexion and dark hair.

"How did you hear about this position, Mason?" I ask, flipping through his resume. Mason has a bachelor's degree in business science and communication—not exactly what I was expecting.

"My aunt, actually. She's a curator at the Guggenheim and always has her fingers on the pulse of what's going on in the art scene of New York." Mason is soft-spoken but firm, with a kind smile that put me at ease.

I raise my eyebrows. "That's a prestigious position."

Mason nods. "She raised me, actually, and it's where I gained my appreciation for art. I worked alongside her as her assistant for a few years but she's ready to retire soon. I know I don't have the educational background some of the other candidates have, but I assure you my real-world experience more than makes up for it, and as you can see my degree does lend itself toward business and a more organizational mindset."

I perk up, reading over his qualifications and job history. He might not be the obvious choice, but so far, he's the first one not to talk my ear off about why he's perfect for the position.

"Do you live in Manhattan?" I ask conversationally, gathering my thoughts.

"Lenox Hill," he confirms. "My husband and I just moved there late last year. The housing market is atrocious right now, as I'm sure you know, and we were very blessed to find the space that we did."

I dive into all the normal interview questions then, and Mason is sweet and easy to talk to. If anything, I'd be concerned that he wouldn't have the hard edge that would be needed to deal with the more persistent, annoying clients I may have to deal with. Towards the end of the interview, I ask Mason if he has questions for me, which he declines, but instead opens his leather messenger bag and hands me a binder to look over. Intrigued, I sit forward and take it from him.

"If you decide I'm the right candidate for your job, I've compiled this schedule and the few things I'd need from you to start forwarding your calls to my business cell. If you look closely, you can see where I've set aside time for us to talk each morning and each evening to go over expectations for the day and then to summarize who I've spoken to throughout. Of course, I'll inform you of any pressing matters, but I know you are currently a student and it's hard for you to answer a call anytime during the day."

"Interesting," I comment, leafing through the binder, at once impressed and overwhelmed by this amount of organization.

"We can use a scheduling platform where we can exchange notes, potential appointments, and anything else you may need without even having to pick up your phone to call. That way, if you think of something in the middle of a lecture, or late at night, you can plug it into the scheduling app, and I'll be informed."

"This is... amazing," I tell him with a nervous laugh. "You really prepared for this interview."

Mason shrugs one shoulder self-consciously. "I've done my own research on you and your gallery, and I have a huge amount of respect for what you're doing for local, emerging artists. As an art lover myself, I'd love to be able to help you thrive. New York needs more fresh blood out there."

The next candidate is going to have to pull a rabbit out of his hat to beat this guy, I think to myself, carefully closing Mason's binder and handing it back to him. "This is very impressive, Mason. I'm sure you'll be hearing back from me. I just have a few more interviews to conduct and then—"

Before I can finish, there is a quiet knock on the door, and without waiting for an answer, Tilly pops her head in. "The reporters are downstairs, but Petra..." she hesitates. "I think they have misled us. They both look to be in their forties, not university journalists at all."

I exchange a confused glance with Mason before standing, straightening myself. "Mr. Palmer, I'll be in touch, I promise," I tell him before following Tilly.

Her warning is making apprehension crawl up my spine, and I want to get to the bottom of who exactly is in my gallery as quickly as I can.

* * *

Halfway down the grand staircase, I can see that Tilly was right, and both reporters are much too old to be working for a university paper. One is tall and chunky with an oily ponytail pulled back from his head, holding a camera, and recording the portion of the gallery that had been set aside for Shiori's paintings. The other looks more put together, with a close-cropped beard and wide-rimmed glasses, and he's whispering to his partner, pointing at some of her artwork.

I can see the last interview candidate standing off to the side looking unsure, as if she can sense something strange in the air, just like I can. I hear Mason a few steps behind me on the stairs, but I'm too weirded out by whatever is going on here to take the time to reassure my potential employees. I need to handle this now.

It just doesn't make sense why they would lie about who they worked for. We weren't currently allowing press in, but every time some reporter called we would let them know press tours would commence in a few weeks. There's nothing at the gallery now that wouldn't be available for viewing then.

The two journalists must have heard the click of my heels on the stairs, because they turn to me as soon as I reach the bottom, like wolves converging on a doe. They give me the creeps immediately, but I have to remind myself I'm the face of this gallery, and if they, by some stretch of the imagination, do work for my college's newspaper, I don't want to appear like I'm alienating anyone.

Tilly's hand settles on my upper arm, and I give her a quick glance. Her gaze is flinty as she watches the men, and I'm given the impression of a hawk keeping a keen eye on a threat. "Just give me the word and I'll phone the police," she tells me under her breath, and I nod curtly. Her hand falls away and I go to confront the journalists.

"Good morning. I see you've found our collection of Shi's paintings. It's our newest installment."

The shorter man with glasses smiles politely, motioning to the wing of the gallery. "It really is an incredible collection for an independently owned gallery. You must be Petra Van Gatt, right?"

I ignore the question. "What paper did you say you were with?"

The man's smile becomes sharper. "Oh, we're freelancers."

I tilt my chin up stubbornly. "Then I'm going to have to ask you to leave. As I'm sure you've heard, we'll be doing press tours in the upcoming weeks. We're only accepting educational tours at the moment."

"Sure, sure," he seems to brush me off, turning back to the art installation and making a discreet motion to his colleague, who hands him a tablet. After a second of flipping, he pulls up a picture on the screen and holds it out for me to see. I bristle when I see that it's a picture from the art auction of Shi and Emma, arm in arm, with me slightly in the background. "Is this you with Emma Hasenfratz at Shi's auction a few weeks ago? It is, right?"

I have to resist the urge to slap the tablet out of the man's hand, but it's then I realize the other man has his camera held up in front of me, seemingly recording us. A chill runs through my spine as I figure what this is all about. "I said you two need to leave. We aren't open to the public today."

The reporter ignores me completely, taking a step forward, while the other man keeps the camera on. I don't step back like I think he expected, but he seems unperturbed. "Why don't you just answer a few questions for me, and I'll be on my way? Where is Emma today? Is she here?"

I try to step past the reporter to his colleague to force him to put the camera down, my heart racing, but the reporter steps in front of me again. "Why won't you answer the questions, Ms. Van Gatt? Is it true you managed to acquire this collection because your friend is sleeping with the artist Shi? This is the biggest collection of her work in the U.S. currently."

"Now, Tilly," I say before turning my attention back to the two men. "I'm gonna need the two of you to get the hell out of my gallery before law enforcement arrives."

Both men laugh. "Such harsh language. Just so you know, we're streaming live, so you might want to watch your mouth."

I cross my arms, trying to look more confident than I'm feeling. I'm all too aware that there is no one in the gallery but Tilly and the two interviewees, but before I can finish the thought, I hear the front door of the gallery opening and the last woman I hadn't gotten a chance to interview slipping out, apparently unwilling to deal with this upheaval. I don't blame her, honestly.

This moment seems unreal. Neither of these men would be intimidating out on the streets, but here, with just myself, my gallery supervisor, and someone I had just interviewed, I feel overwhelmed by them. The fact that they are streaming makes it even worse, as I have no idea how wide their audience is or how many people are watching me try to keep the fear off my face right in this second.

"Just answer a few questions for us, Petra, and we'll be on our way." The reporter's voice is slimy as he moves forward to try and crowd me again. "That, or maybe you could get us an interview with your friend Emma."

"I'm not telling you anything, sir, and my gallery supervisor has just called law enforcement, so I'd suggest you be on your way."

He snorts. "You think the police in Manhattan are going to make two reporters in an art gallery a priority? It's New York, sweetie. This entire city is crawling with reporters."

A shudder runs through me, thinking about the paparazzi back in Aspen, and how what he's saying just might be true. I'm sorely regretting telling Zach to go home and wait on my call, because he'd have been able to muster some of Alex's security team in minutes. Right now, I'm cursing myself for leaving my cell phone upstairs, and my patience with these two is running thin.

The reporter takes my silence as an invitation to continue speaking, and his colleague holds the camera closer to me. "We've got insider information saying that Shi is holding a private exhibit in Tokyo Sunday and there's a jet out of Teterboro to Tokyo booked on Friday. Is Emma Hasenfratz going to the exhibit in Tokyo with Shi? Is she going as a friend, collector, or maybe lover? What can you tell us about that, Petra?"

"Absolutely nothing," I grit out. "Now get out of my gallery!"

Both men laugh again, and I can feel my cheeks burning with embarrassment. "Speaking of gallery, why did your husband decide to gift it to you? Was it to make up for you spending most of your pregnancy alone, is that so?"

I'm rocked by the sudden shift in the questioning, moving to focus on me, and I'm suddenly awash in memories of all the press during Alex's court case and how miserable we had all been. For the first time, I take a nervous step backward, shaking my head. I'm ready to flee, but I can't.

Like the bird of prey I had compared her to earlier, Tilly swoops past me and locks her hands on the upper arm of the reporter, causing him to startle. "That's enough!" Tilly hisses. "Both of you lowlifes get out of this gallery right this second."

I watch, terrified, as the cameraman moves quickly as if he's going to bat Tilly off his friend. Before he can, though, Mason steps in and grabs his arm just as Tilly did to the reporter. The cameraman is taller and stouter, but Mason is strong enough to hold his ground, and both men stop in their tracks when he enters their space.

"I'd suggest you leave," Mason says evenly. "Ms. Petra here was conducting some business before you so rudely interrupted. Lying to get into the gallery was a dirty move, don't you think? As if the two of you could ever pass for college students."

All while making this speech, Mason is hauling the cameraman toward the door, who seems shocked enough to stumble along behind him. The reporter, on the other hand, tries to shake Tilly off, but her nails are dug firmly into his arm and her expression is stubborn and unmovable. She's at least five inches taller than the man in her heels, and despite him trying to pull away, she manages to walk him to the door too.

Mason pushes the door open with his hip and all but throws the cameraman out, and Tilly follows suit, pushing the reporter between the shoulder blades and slamming the lock into place as the door shuts behind them. The gallery is suddenly silent.

I let out a shaking breath, and then a nervous laugh, laying my hand over my galloping heart. "Thank you both," I tell them sincerely.

"I know this is your gallery, Petra, but it's mine to supervise, and I'll be damned if some skeezy beat reporters are going to intimidate you or disrespect the artwork that these artists poured their hearts and souls into," Tilly huffs, and although she looks cooly confidant, I see a flicker of unease on her face.

I turn to Mason, planning to offer an even more heartfelt apology to this young man I had just met and who came to the defense of me and my precious gallery, but he holds up a hand as soon as I open my mouth. "No thanks necessary. Growing up, I had to deal with my fair share of bullies, and I have no tolerance for them now. They meant to intimidate you, and I'm glad I was here to help. I'd have done it no matter who you were." He levels a serious gaze at me. "It wasn't some ploy to guarantee myself the job. I hope you know."

"Absolutely," I tell him. "But you have to know you've shot to the top of the pack."

He grins and shrugs a single shoulder. "I'll take any positive karma that comes my way."

I escort Mason upstairs so he can get the bag he had brought with him, and I grab my phone as he gets his things together.

Mason is ready to leave, but right before he reaches his hand toward the front door handle, Tilly stops him. "Wait a second," she cautions. "The police still aren't here, and I have a bad feeling they might still be outside."

She pulls up the security camera app on her phone, and when she brings up the feed for the front door camera, both the reporter and the cameraman are in fact still standing on the stairs, arms crossed and waiting patiently for one of us to come out. No doubt to harangue us with more questions, but it still gives me a shudder to see them waiting.

Thankfully, though, just a few minutes later, we watch on the tiny screen as a lone police car pulls up. At the sight of it, both men casually descend the steps of the gallery to leave, hands shoved in their pockets as if they are nothing more than sight seers walking the streets of Manhattan. The officer pays them no mind, coming to the gallery door and knocking.

Tilly lets the officer in, and bidding Mason goodbye, we give the officer a rundown of everything that happened. The moment he takes out his pad of paper to make the report, though, the gallery phone begins to ring. Followed by my cellphone. And then Tilly's cellphone.

Pulling my phone out of my pocket, I see in place of the number just the word "private." Tilly holds hers up, and it reads the same. All three phones stop ringing, and then immediately start again.

"Answer it, on speaker," the officer instructs.

With a gulp, I do as he says, and a voice rings in the empty gallery among the sounds of the other ringing phones.

"Hello, is this Petra Van Gatt? I'm calling from Page Eight media—"

I hang up immediately, pinching the bridge of my nose and uttering an uncharacteristic curse.

"Shit."

CHAPTER 3

Petra

We field calls for hours. I didn't even know there were so many ways to say "no comment" or so many newspaper and press companies in New York City. By the time the calls stopped coming in, and Tilly and I had managed to block as many as we could from our personal phones. Now it's nearly 5 pm, and we are both beyond over it. At least my office got its first full day of use.

Tilly, exhausted, goes to do her evening walkthrough of the gallery to make sure nothing is amiss, and I take the opportunity to check the gallery's social media pages, which I immediately regret. I have over one hundred message requests, probably more, but the app seems to stop counting after a hundred. I don't even glance through them, just hold my finger down and let the screen scroll and scroll, selecting all the messages and deleting them en masse. I don't care if it's Queen Elizabeth herself messaging me on Instagram.

There is not a single person outside of my small social circle I'm interested in talking with.

Once Tilly confirms everything is where it should be, I call Zach to come and pick me up, instructing him to come to the front door, and he and I would walk Tilly to her cab before leaving.

Of course, there is one person I shouldn't keep ignoring— my husband. He tried to call me twice earlier and sent a text afterwards. I know with each passing minute that it sits unanswered in my inbox is another level of worry that'll encompass Alex. I just don't have it in me to go over the entire ordeal through a phone call, and honestly, I want to be with him when I explain everything. He might already be furious about the whole ordeal, so I think it'll be better if he can see with his own two eyes that I am safe and sound.

In the car's backseat, with my familiar driver at the wheel and the doors locked, I can take my first deep breath in over six hours. I'm so twisted up inside from everything. Guilt weighs heavily on me, knowing that I had subjected my only employee to this nonsense today, and that my favorite pick for my new personal assistant might have been spooked away. There are so many things I could have done to prevent that disaster from happening, so many tiny things like telling Zach to stay waiting for me outside, or even taking my phone with me downstairs.

Jeez! What if the twins had been there with me? There are plenty of days I had brought them to work with me, letting them bounce in their bouncers, or having one strapped to my chest in their sling while Emma or Alex carted the other around. I had wanted the gallery to be their home away from home, and I had been seriously considering children's art classes, or even mommy and me classes... but what if it wasn't safe for children to be in my gallery, because there were crazy, relentless people like the reporters today always around?

I shiver, wrapping my arms tightly around my body and screwing my eyes shut. Today had sent so many cracks through all of my carefully laid plans for the gallery, and I'm not yet sure how to fix it. And all that was because of Emma and Shi? It isn't even my relationship or my drama to talk about for Pete's sake! I laugh sardonically to myself, thinking about how, in some way, this was all my fault. If I hadn't told Margaret about her daughter's affair, she'd have never commanded me to deal with the Yara and Emma debacle, and none of this would have happened.

Still, though. I can't say I'm not happy for Emma and the way she is breaking the chains of her toxic relationship, or for my personal and professional friendship with Shi. There are upsides and downsides to it all. It's just complicated.

Complicated, and so scary.

Zach doesn't say a word once we arrive at the condo. He simply steps out of the car, opens my door, and escorts me to the front door. It's an unusual gesture but I appreciate the security his presence gives me, even if he's just my driver. As I come to think of it, Zach is Alex's employee, and if I know my husband at all, he probably has a gun tucked somewhere on his person and extensive training with it, just in case.

Lily is doing flashcards with the twins when I walk in, and she gives me an understanding look. *Great.* I guess everyone already knows my business, including my kids' nurse. Jasmine and Jasper immediately ignore Lily's cards when they catch sight of me, and it's a relief to hold them both in my arms and bury my face in their little necks, feeling how warm and soft and blessedly safe they are. It brings a lump to my throat.

"Alex is in his office," Lily says gently, plucking Jasmine from my grasp. "He wanted to talk to you when you got home."

I give her an annoyed look and sink down onto the couch instead. Jasper pulls himself up, his hands clutching the couch fabric, and looks at me with eyes the same color as his father's, huffing and puffing with the effort of holding himself up.

"Great job, buddy," I tell him, pulling him up into my lap, ignoring Lily, who continues to stare at me.

"Petra," she starts.

"I know," I blurt out in a whisper. "I know he wants to see me, and from the look on your face, you know what it's about. Just give me a second, please."

Lily lowers herself down next to me and lays a gentle hand on my knee. She always radiates calm, quiet energy, and even I, as an adult, am not immune to it. I finally relent, sliding my gaze over to her.

"I'm going to tell you what I know, so you don't have to hear it from your very distressed husband. The video that the reporters live streamed was all over Twitter, and right before you came in, they played it on TMZ Live. Alex has seen the entire thing, and he's setting up a security force for you, at least that's from what I can tell."

I blanch, simultaneously pulling my earring out of Jasper's searching hand. "Their livestream was played on *cable television?*"

Lily winces in sympathy. "At least you looked absolutely radiant." She tugs on the edge of my blouse. "This color is incredible with your complexion."

With a heavy sigh, I hand the other woman my wiggling son, and stand. "I guess I should go speak to him and see how exactly he plans on changing my life to fit his parameters."

"He's just trying to keep you and the kids safe, Petra," Lily chides. "Whatever security measures he insists on can only be beneficial. This will all die down soon enough."

I'm unconvinced, but she doesn't need to know that, so instead I give her a small smile and say, "I hope you're right."

* * *

Alex is in his office, just like Lily said, leaning back in his chair with his tie loosened and top shirt buttons undone. He's on a phone call when I enter, and he holds up a finger to let me know he'll be with me in just a second. I take a seat on the leather loveseat against the wall and wait.

It's clear Alex has been dragging his fingers through his hair ceaselessly because it's sticking up in all different directions, and he looks like he's been pushed to his limits. He has been so hands off with my mission to get Emma away from Yara that it's almost shocking considering how protective he is, but I know this would be different. Even

Yara and her vague threats of violence are a known factor. Strangers are a different story.

Alex hangs up his phone and scrubs his hands over his face with a groan. I bet he's been at this since the moment he got home. I open my mouth to ask him what he wanted to talk about, but instead he stands and walks over to the couch to sit next to me, pulling me into his embrace without a word.

Until that very second, I didn't know quite how much I needed him, and I feel tears gathering at the corner of my eyes. I take a ragged breath and push myself as close to him as I can get, letting him run his hands up and down my back comfortingly as I fight back tears.

After a few long moments, I sit up a little straighter and wipe my eyes. "Sorry. I shouldn't be crying. Nothing bad really happened."

Alex sighs. "It was bad, Petra. Have you seen the video?" I shake my head, and he pulls out his iPhone. I start to protest but he interrupts me. "I need you to watch it before I ask you the questions I need to ask. I want you to know exactly what we are dealing with."

"I was literally there," I tell him. "I don't need to relive it."

"You need to see what the rest of the world is seeing if you're going to make the right decisions."

The thought of watching the video makes me nauseous, but finally I nod, and Alex pulls it up.

It's as horrible as I thought, watching myself get more and more flustered by the reporters, and how it was Tilly and Mason who finally had to throw them out, not me, the owner of the freaking gallery! From the perspective of the reporters, they appeared to be thrown out almost violently, instead of the barely won struggle it had actually been, and it made me go cold. They were obviously trying to change the narrative to make themselves into the victims and me as someone unreasonable and unhinged.

I shudder against Alex once he closes the video, and I let out a shaking exhale. "That was awful."

"You did well, all things considered," Alex reassures me. "You didn't give them a single scrap of information."

"It didn't seem to deter them."

"They were trying to rattle you enough that you let something slip," he explains.

I don't answer, choosing instead to snuggle with my husband, hoping we can let the subject go for the moment. I should've known better though, knowing Alex.

He untangles himself from me and goes to his desk, coming back with a stack of papers.

"First," he asks. "Who was the other man at the gallery that helped your supervisor?"

There's the slightest edge to his voice, nothing that anyone but me would have noticed. Despite everything, a tiny smile pulls at the corner of my mouth. "Jealous?"

Alex just looks at me, unamused.

"Fine," I say. "His name is Mason, and he was one of the candidates for the PA job I interviewed today."

Alex shuffles through his pile of papers and pulls out a copy of Mason's resume. I'm not surprised since he had been the one to print out my copies and organize the interviews for me.

"This one?" he asks, and I nod.

After reading the resume carefully, Alex hums to himself, tucking the sheet of paper back into the pile. "I'm impressed with his tenacity and his willingness to go to bat for you. Did you like him?"

"Actually," I pull at the edge of my blouse nervously, wondering if Alex is going to think I'm being too hasty. "I have more interviews scheduled tomorrow, but I honestly just want to hire Mason. He has everything I'm looking for in a PA, and he even recommended a few apps we can use to keep everything organized."

Alex shrugs. "Hire him, then. His first task can be canceling your interviews for tomorrow."

I giggle unexpectedly. "Alex! I can't have my personal assistant cancel my other personal assistant interviews!"

"Why not?" he asks, his voice even. "Sometimes, as a business owner, you just have employees that click into place naturally. This Mason seems like that for you, so let's put him on the payroll. In fact..." Alex pulls something else out of his massive paper pile, and I realize it's a check. "I had this written out for whoever it was that helped you as a tip. You can tell him to consider it a hire-on bonus."

I take the check gingerly from between his fingers, folding it and tucking it into my jeans pocket. "Okay... I guess I will when we're done?"

"Great. Now, this is serious, Petra, so pay attention."

"I am," I say, with a hint of annoyance. Did he think I was off in space or something?

"Good, and don't argue with what I'm about to tell you." Alex clears his throat. "We're going to sue the fuck out of those reporters."

I sort of knew this was coming, but I still pinch the bridge of my nose between my fingers and groan.

"Alex, no. I just want this to go away, not chase it down."

"You don't understand," he starts, "if we let this slide, it will set a precedent for other people like them to harass you without consequences. Do you want them following you to work every day? School? Out for a walk with the kids?"

"Of course not!" I fight the urge to jump up and pace the floor. "But there's also an argument for giving the situation more attention and energy drawing in more reporters."

Alex doesn't seem deterred. "I've already spoken to my lawyers about everything, and it's a slam dunk case for defamation and harassment. You won't even have to be very involved, just give your statement and they can take care of the rest."

"We don't even know who they are, though. They told me they were freelancers."

He shakes his head. "Well, they are and they aren't. They publish their own stories, but they do it under the umbrella of a shady media corporation. We have names of the reporter, the cameraman, and the company who buys their stories. We've already done all the work. Like I said, all you have to do is agree and I'll take it from here."

I want to argue more, because I want so badly to put all of this behind me, but a large part of me knows that Alex is right. If we let this go away without consequences for them, it might be seen as an invitation for other reporters to do the same.

"Fine," I acquiesce. "I don't like it, but if you insist…"

"I do." Alex drops his stack of papers on the desk and goes back to sit beside me, putting two fingers under my chin and tilting my gaze up to his. "You know I wouldn't do anything to make you uncomfortable unless I really thought it was necessary. Everything I do is to protect you, Jasmine, and Jasper."

"I know," I tell him, shoulders sagging. "I'm just so tired of all of this. I want to go back to our peaceful, drama-free existence."

"It won't be like this forever. You just have the unfortunate honor of being best friends with the girlfriend of the media's current darling artist. They'll find someone else to fawn over soon enough, especially if Emma and Shi get into a serious relationship. They want upheaval, not the average, happy couple."

"If you say so." I'm unconvinced, but all I want right now is to put this whole story behind me.

"I do." He cups my face, affection clear in his gaze. "I promise I won't lead you astray."

"Now that that's settled–" I say hopefully, but Alex shakes his head. I sigh. "More?"

"Yes, more. We need to talk about your security."

"Then let me lay down, at least. I'm exhausted."

We shuffle around on the couch, and I kick off my heels, calves dangling over the arm of the leather loveseat and my head pillowed in Alex's lap. He cards his fingers through my hair soothingly, and I wonder if he will notice if I fall asleep. There's no such luck, though.

"I've got my normal security personnel, but I've also got a small squad still on retainer from the court case last year that

I plan on activating to guard the gallery when it's open, even if you aren't there. It will be their only job, so you won't have to worry about them splitting up their attention and getting distracted."

"Good," I murmur, my eyes fluttering closed.

"For your own personal security, I'm going to reassign some of my personal guards. I have a great guy, Pascal, who will be the head of your personal team. I'll introduce you to him tomorrow."

"Lovely," I mutter, nearly dozing off.

I can feel Alex focus his attention on me again. "Petra, you need to pay attention."

"I am, I am," I insist, not opening my eyes. "I'm just resting."

"Uh-huh…." Alex doesn't argue, though, continuing on, "Listen, I know you're upset about all of this, but I don't want you to downplay how serious it all is. Do you know how many views their original video got?"

"A couple thousand?" I ask, an ounce of humor trailing on my lips.

His hand stills in my hair. "Baby… It was a couple million."

My eyes shoot open, meeting Alex's sympathetic cerulean gaze. "Million? Holy moly."

"Holy moly is right," he sighs, before starting to thread his fingers against my scalp again. It's a comforting touch, and it takes the sting out of everything he's revealing to me. "That's why it's so much more likely you'll be recognized out on the streets. You're going to have a constant security detail until I feel like this has died down enough that you aren't endangered anymore. The detail will be doubled when you're out with the kids."

"By a constant detail, you don't mean at school, right? Columbia has their own security, there's nothing to worry about."

"Constant means *constant*, love. Even at Columbia." Despite his tone being sympathetic, I'm not sold on the idea.

I suppress an outright complaint, instead just telling him, "Alex, you don't know how humiliating that will be. School is the only time I feel like a normal woman my age, around my peers. I don't want a constant reminder hanging around that I'm different."

"I promise you they'll be as discreet as possible. You won't even notice they are there unless you want to. I suggest making them a little more obvious when you're out in public, but we can have them be almost invisible at Columbia, if that's what you want. Reluctantly, I do trust Columbia's security enough to believe they won't let reporters and paparazzi on the grounds."

"Hmm," I peek up at him again. "You already called them, didn't you?"

He chuckles. "You know me too well."

Alex lets the conversation die off, knowing that he's gotten the agreement out of me that he wanted. I'm too emotionally drained, and too fed up with the whole situation to really argue, and it was sort of a weight off of my shoulders to let Alex take control of everything. And as I know all too well, Alex loves to be in control.

I know I have two children downstairs I should go and be with, and a media firestorm to address, but for the moment I don't want to do anything but fall into that half-sleep state with my head on my husband's lap. His office smells of paper, ink, and his cologne, and being with each other has obviously eased both of our anxieties over the past eight or so hours. My limbs feel loose and relaxed, and here with Alex, I can shut out the real world for a minute.

He lets me,   seemingly lost in his own thoughts. I understand how he feels. The stakes are so much higher now than they were before, and the situations are so much more nuanced. This moment alone is a reprieve before a storm of chaos, and I think we both know it.

I've drifted off just enough to shut everything else out when my phone rings. My first instinct is to ignore it, but Alex has other ideas, picking it up from where I had left it on the floor by my shoes. I'm positive it's another paper or reporter that slipped through the number blocking cracks from earlier, but to my surprise, it's a contact I already have saved on my phone.

When he shows me the screen and I see it's Shiori, I know exactly why she's calling me. The gossip mill in Tokyo might not be as interested in what had happened to me today, but Shiori lives half her life in Manhattan, so she had to have her finger on the pulse of the goings on around here. I reluctantly push myself to a sitting position and answer the phone.

"Petra," Shiori says immediately, sounding subdued. "My PR team has just informed me of what happened today at your gallery, and I wanted to call and personally apologize."

Shiori is a secretive woman, and over our time in St. Moritz, I slowly discovered her anonymity was to protect a gentle, kind heart. Of course she'd feel some sort of responsibility over what happened.

"It's not even vaguely your fault, Shi. You're in Tokyo! You don't need to apologize."

"I do, though," Shiori replies. "If it wasn't for how high-profile Emma and I have been over the past few weeks, you would never have been bothered like that."

"That's not true," I assure her. "Either way, I have your paintings in the gallery, and I've got the only real collection of your work in the city right now."

"You and I both know that those reporters weren't interested in my work. They were interested in my love life." She scoffs, sounding hurt, "All of my career I've tried to hide away, so I'd be judged only by my work. As soon as I show my face, all anyone wants to talk to me about is my identity, and who I'm seeing. I feel like no one even cares about my art anymore."

I'm silent for a second, worried that Shi is regretting everything with Emma already, especially knowing that the attention that is currently being heaped on me will switch over to her if she returns to Manhattan. "I'm sure Emma didn't–"

"You misunderstand," Shiori interrupts. "I willingly go through this because I want her. I want Emma, as bizarre as it sounds after only knowing her for such a short time, and I always strive for what I want. No amount of media attention is going to change my mind, but I never expected that media attention would affect my friends like it has affected you today. And for that, I apologize, whether you accept my apology or not."

Shiori is wavering between indignation and vulnerability, and I'm touched that she considers me a friend. "Shi," I say gently. "Of course I accept your apology, even if I think it's unnecessary."

She exhales and sounds lighter, as if she's unburdened herself of something. "Thank you. Petra?"

"Yes?"

"Have… have you talked to Emma today?"

"No," I admit. "She's texted me, but I've just been too busy to reply."

"Understandable," Shiori says.

"Has she accepted your invitation yet?" I ask hopefully.

Her voice is sad as she responds. "No, not yet. I thought she had cut her ties from your sister-in-law, but I guess her claws are in Emma deeper than I expected." Shiori is quiet for a second, as if she's thinking something over. "Why does she stay with her? Emma has an open heart that is waiting for love, but she's also so intelligent. I'd have never expected her to be so attached to someone as toxic as Yara."

I laugh, and it's tinged with frustration. "I totally agree. It's gonna take time, but I'm sure she'll move on."

"She will come," Shiori says confidently, any uncertainty that was in her voice earlier dissipating. "I am sure of it."

"I really hope you're right…."

"I have everything planned out. I want to show her how good a relationship based not just on chemistry, but on mutual respect can be." Shiori sighs, but the sound is laced with hope. "She will come."

We talk a little longer while Alex straightens up his desk and shoots out a few emails. Shi tells me that if there's anything she can do to take some of the pressure off me, to just let her know. I'm reluctant to ask for her help, knowing how private she is, but having the option is a small comfort.

After I hang up, I consider calling Emma and grilling her. Not about the events of today, but whether she's going to take up Shiori's invitation. In the end, I decided not to. She has to be the one to decide, or it won't mean as much.

Well, if Emma goes, and she and Shiori become official, all this nonsense will have been worth it.

* * *

After dinner, I'm well and done with the day, but I've still got one last task to do before going to bed—calling Mason to let him know he got the job.

A few minutes later, I find myself on a long video call with my new personal assistant, going over the details of the plan for the next days. I must have looked frazzled, because Mason, who I'm still on a video call with, leans toward the camera and blinks.

"No offense, boss, but you look like you're about to fall asleep on the keyboard."

I roll my neck, stretching the stiff muscles. "I don't think I'm that far gone yet."

"Mmhm…" He doesn't seem to believe me but continues. "Can I ask a question?"

I look up from the pile of documents in front of me, where I had been filling out his basic information to finalize the hiring process. "Of course."

"You're not just hiring me because I got involved at the gallery today, are you? If you're worried about me expecting something from you and your husband, monetarily or whatever else, I—"

"Well, it certainly sealed the deal for you, but you were my favorite candidate prior to that incident," I assure him. "It's not a guilt thing, though. Promise. But are you sure you want to work for me, knowing how insane everything can be around here?"

Mason gives me a small smile and looks over his shoulder as if he's confirming he's alone. "I don't mind kicking a few reporters out. It makes for a fun drama story to tell my husband back home."

I snort. "Maybe a few years ago I'd have agreed, but I think my drama tolerance meter has run out."

"Well, I'll soak it all up for you and enjoy every minute of it." Mason smiles wider, his brilliantly white teeth flashing. "While remaining unflinchingly professional, of course."

Jeez, I might have my hands full with this one. But honestly, I needed a big personality. Someone who wouldn't pull the punches when dealing with my clients, but who would also be completely real with me when I'm being indecisive.

I pick the papers up, tapping the pile on the desk and setting them aside. "We can hammer out a decision on your salary and I'll have you on the payroll tomorrow. How do you feel about starting tonight, though? Remotely, of course." I check the time, and it's somehow only 8 pm. Not too late to call off my other interviews tomorrow.

"As long as I can log the hours, I'm more than happy to. What do you need?"

I give him the rundown of the three candidates I need him to call and cancel, and Mason seems to lighten up as he takes his own notes. Either he really did love drama, or he was truly excited to get the job... My bet is on a little bit of both.

"Tell them that we'll be hiring other positions as the year goes on. Art dealers, tour guides, etcetera, so if they want to be the first ones called when we do, we're more than happy to do so. For the inconvenience of canceling on such short notice, of course."

"Sure, sure." Mason closes his notebook, putting the pencil he was using behind his ear. "I'll get right on it. Are you sure you won't need me tomorrow morning?"

"I don't even know what I would have you do, honestly. It's going to be damage control for the next few days, but I'll get a hold of you when I figure myself out."

He chuckles, seeming to understand how stretched thin I was. "Get some rest, boss. I'll talk to you soon."

I check the baby monitor app on my phone as soon as we hang up, watching Alex tuck the twins into their cribs despite their wiggly, loud protests. He had promised me he'd get them to bed, and that I didn't need to worry about anything else tonight, but seeing him being the amazing father he has always been makes something squeeze in my chest.

I stand, stretching my arms high over my head until the stiff muscles in my back give way, relaxing at last. With that, I go to join my husband in the nursery, knowing that despite everything that happened today, I don't want to miss a single second with my family.

CHAPTER 4

Manhattan, February 2, 2022
Petra

Alex rolls over as the sunrise streams through the glass of our windows, bathing the room in warm, yellow light despite the time of the year. Logically, I know the streets would be slushy, and the air would be frigid, but here, storeys above the city, it's easy to pretend that everything in the city is as beautiful as the morning sun.

He pulls me into the cradle of his body, his warm breath stirring my hair where it lay over my neck. We are skin-to-skin, always sleeping with as few clothes on as possible, especially now that the twins mostly slept through the night. Even in sleep, we crave the feeling of each other's skin.

"Good morning, wife," he rumbles, and I huff in protest. Maybe if he doesn't acknowledge it's daytime, we can stay in bed a little longer. "Let's go shower, both of us," he tries, which gets a response out of me, albeit still a wordless one. I hum in agreement, scooching my body even further into the curve of his.

"Lazy," he jokes, nibbling the sleep-warm skin of my nape, causing me to squeal and try to push him away. He holds me tight, laughing, until I settle.

"Fine, I'm awake!"

"Good," he purrs. "Let's have a long and luxurious shower, and maybe a detour back between the sheets once we're clean...."

"That sounds like it will take all day," I tease.

"I can be quick if I need to be. But don't worry," he nips at my neck again, and this time, I shiver. "I'm always thorough, wife."

Alex is, indeed, thorough, and by the time he has carried me from beneath the steaming shower, panting and needy, I'm more than ready to do whatever it is he desires. He tosses me, my long hair still dripping water, unceremoniously on the bed, causing the air to blow out of my lungs in a laugh.

"How much longer do we have?" he growls, jumping onto the bed and grabbing me around my bare waist.

I have no idea. Five minutes? An hour? Who cares? I had forever for him. "As long as we need," I respond, my voice thick and sultry, and Alex's smile is both triumphant and just a bit dangerous.

* * *

We do have breakfast together later than is probably appropriate for two working parents, but both of us had worked up a considerable appetite. I don't have class today, but I need to meet Tilly at the gallery to go over the new security protocols before we open for the public. I have no doubt that we will be busier than ever, both with Shi's exhibit and the media mess yesterday.

Thankfully, Tilly doesn't seem bothered when I message her, letting her know I'd be late. After all, she had opened the gallery on her own plenty of times before. So I try to enjoy my breakfast, oatmeal with fresh berries, dodging Jasmine's grabbing hands when I waited too long to give her a bite. At one point I'm distracted, talking to Maria as she putters around the kitchen about what dinners sounded good for the week, and Jasmine takes the opportunity to yank the spoon from my hand with all of her strength, cramming it immediately into her mouth to gum on.

"Enough out of you, little miss, you need to be patien–oh my goodness! Alex!" I yell, gently prying the spoon from her fingers before pulling her bottom lip down for a quick look. I had only glimpsed the little white spot on her gums before, but now I am sure—my little girl is getting her first tooth! No wonder she's been extra fussy.

Alex hustles over, and I show him my discovery. We're both giddy, me probably a little more so, and I snap approximately one hundred pictures to send to my dad, Emma, and everyone else I even vaguely care about in my contact list.

Jasper is less than thrilled when I try to peek in his mouth, but I'm able to slide a quick finger over his bottom gums when he opens his mouth for a bite of oatmeal, looking for all the world like a baby bird. He doesn't have any visible teeth yet, but the hard bumps on his otherwise soft gums are unmistakable.

"We need to make a trip to the baby shop and get some teething supplies," I warn. "None of this alcohol on the gums like my dad keeps telling me to do."

"We'll make a list tonight, as long as nothing else crazy happens today," Alex says distractedly, responding to something on his phone. I know he had to leave work early yesterday after his PR people sent him the video of me, and he's already later going in than he usually is. It's not like he really has anyone to answer to, but he's an integral part of the company, and I'm sure his presence is sorely missed when he isn't around.

Selfishly, though, I'm not ready for either of us to leave for the day. Once we walk out the front door, the consequences of yesterday's mess would begin. I'm sure to have a full day of fielding calls and making sure anyone entering the gallery is simply a guest, and not an undercover journalist or someone trying to take advantage of the situation for social media clout.

I'm just contemplating calling Tilly and telling her we will remain closed to the public for the rest of the week when my phone screen lights up. Coincidentally, it's my gallery supervisor herself calling. I expect her to tell me she's able to open the gallery without an issue, but when I answer, I can hear a cacophony of voices.

"Petra!" Tilly seems to yell over a crowd. "We've got a problem! The front of the gallery and the surrounding sidewalks are completely filled with news agencies and reporters! I can't even get up the steps to unlock the door. What do you want me to do?"

Alex must have been able to see the alarm on my face because he is immediately standing next to me, asking me in a whisper about what is going on. I gesture at him to wait.

"Have you called the police yet?"

"Yes. They're on their way, but they can't stay here forever. We both know that. What are we going to do?" Tilly keeps asking, her concerns rising.

"Just sit tight and let me talk to Alex. Where are you right now?"

"I'm heading back to my Uber, parked on the curb. The driver is fine running up the meter while we wait here, but if I don't get to go in soon, then I'll either have to brave the streets or go home." She sounds perturbed, and frightened.

"We'll be there soon. Please stay in the car." I make her promise that she won't try to enter the gallery without some sort of escort. It'd be almost nothing for someone to push themselves inside with her, and once the dam is broken, everyone could get inside.

I tell Alex what is going on and show him the picture of the horde of reporters that Tilly sent me. Alex purses his lips, his eyes narrowing. He looks pissed off and dangerous. "We'll handle it," he tells me simply, and before I can ask any questions he's walked away, already dialing someone on the phone. He pauses long enough to tell me to get ready to leave, and then he's gone, making plans that would allow us to make it through the day. I'm curious what exactly he has up his sleeve.

* * *

Arriving at the gallery feels more like arriving at a movie premiere, except in the middle of the street at ten in the morning, Alex is already tense beside me, but I keep reminding myself that we just have to get inside, and everything will settle down.

We've taken two blacked out SUVs, the second one loaded with Alex's security force. At first the crowds don't seem to want to move enough for us to pull up to the curb, but after the drivers lay on the horns and inch their way forward, the tide of people move aside enough for us to park.

We watch out the tinted windows as two of the security guards approach the car that Tilly is in, and once they have made it there, Alex and I get out of our car. The questions and yelling are instantaneous, and I instinctively lower my head as we walk, flanked by the guards. The short distance from the curb to the door of the gallery seems like miles. Our pace is slow, with our guards having to physically move people as we go, but after what seems like forever, we finally make it inside.

Tilly, being the less interesting target, had been able to get inside before Alex and me. She lets out one shaky breath with her shoulders hunched before ditching any nerves from the experience and donning her usual haughty persona.

"That was certainly something," she comments. "I'm assuming we will not be opening for business today?"

"Not as long as they are all out there," I confirm, sadly. "What else can I do?"

"Don't fret," Tilly replies. "I'll head to my office and field phone calls for the day. Would you like me to post a message on the gallery's social media accounts letting the public know we won't be opening?"

"Uh, sure. Can you let me know if any calls you take seem particularly out of the ordinary?"

"Absolutely. I'll use the same message for pushy journalists, too. It can be our official statement about the entire ordeal."

"Perfect."

Now, though, I'm not sure what I'm supposed to do with myself. The gallery has been sitting, waiting to open to the public for days now, and our spotty open/closed schedule definitely didn't look good if we wanted to appear as a serious and professional business.

I'm left standing in the foyer, with Alex at my side and eight guards scattered around us. "Are you going in to work now?"

"Later. First, I'm going to walk through the place with the security people and work out the best plan of action for keeping everyone here safe, including visitors."

I frown. "I don't want you to mess up your work schedule for me."

"Nonsense. If Roy can't run the ship without me for an hour or two, then maybe it's time for him to retire." Alex's tone is light, and I know he's trying not to bog me down with negativity.

"Okay," I say reluctantly. "So, um… what do you think I should do?"

Alex considers it for a moment, taking off his blazer and rolling up his sleeves to prepare for the walkthrough as he does so. "I know you will not like this, but I think you need to call in a favor."

Not sure what he means, I cross my arms. "What favor? With whom?"

"I overheard you and Shiori talking last night, and she told you she would do anything you needed her to do if it would take the heat off of you. I think you should ask her to make a public statement to draw everyone's eyes to her, instead of you."

I don't like the idea, and I rub my temples as I consider it. "Alex... you know she's one of the most private people I know. Asking her to do that would go completely against the grain and make her uncomfortable."

Alex waves his arms toward the crowd outside. "And *this* isn't making *us* uncomfortable?"

Scowling, I reply, "It's apples and oranges, Alex. You can't compare the two."

"I can, and I will. Her making a statement, no matter how private she is, is nothing compared to you being harassed day in and day out. Make the call, Petra."

I really don't want to. Shi had offered to help, but upsetting her risked our professional relationship and her budding romance with Emma. Deep down, though, I know Alex is right. What kind of professional relationship could I have with any artist if I couldn't even open the doors of my gallery?

"Okay, okay. I'll go call her," I relent, and Alex's face softens.

He draws me into him and lays his lips on my forehead in a gentle, comforting kiss. "Thank you. I know I don't know her, but I think she'll be more open to the idea than you think."

I skim my fingers up the lines of his bare forearms before he pulls away. Alright, I get it, time to go and make the phone call.

As I head upstairs, I notice the lights are already on in my office, and to my great pleasure, there's a steaming cup of green tea in a cardboard cup resting on my desk. Bless Tilly. It seemed silly for a workplace with only two employees, but our little break room nook had one very important item: a Keurig, and Tilly and I both put it to good use.

Settling into my chair, I cross my ankles and roll forward, opening my laptop carefully. Almost as if there is a snake hiding inside. I'm really not looking forward to what I will find in my email. But then, I have a thought. I don't need to parse through these emails, do I? I have a personal assistant for that now.

I'm not so naïve that I don't even have a business email set up that's separate from my personal and school addresses, but I'd still need to set up automatic forwarding for Mason. For now, though, I simply selected the 247 emails I had received since yesterday morning on my Gatt-Dieren Galley address and forwarded them manually to my PA.

I send him a text that simply says, *Start logging hours and then check your email. Thanks!*

He replies almost instantly. *You've got it. Need me to come into the gallery?*

Only if you can't do it remotely. I think for a second before adding, *our "official statement" to the press is on our social media pages. You can use it for any communications if you need to. Don't deviate from the official statement much if you can help it.*

Got it.

All the notification bubbles disappearing definitely takes a load off of my shoulders. Curious, I search the gallery name on Instagram so I can read whatever statement has been released. There are only a handful of other pictures, and while they are pleasant to look at with polite, albeit generic, captions, I realize I need to hire another position: a social media manager. I sip my tea, making a note in my endless to-do list to interview for that position before checking out our statement. It's short and straight to the point, and thankfully free of any flowery language that could be easily misconstrued.

Please note that the Gatt-Dieren Gallery will be temporarily closed for an indeterminate amount of time. This will allow us to set up proper measures to address an influx of new guests and implement security protocols to keep our valued visitors safe.

We apologize for the inconveniences caused and appreciate your understanding.

If you have any other questions, please check our website for more information.

I've stalled long enough, though. After flipping through the gallery's Instagram a few more times and jotting down a few ideas to make the engagement better online, I realize I'm really going to have to call Shiori. I do some quick math, cringing when I conclude that it's nearly midnight in Tokyo.

I send her a text first to make sure she's awake. Half of me is hoping she doesn't answer.

Much to my chagrin, she calls me almost immediately and seems perfectly awake and cheery. "Oh, you know us artists. We keep strange hours," she tells me when I apologize for the late time. "What do you need?"

Well, there's no turning back now. "So, I actually think I do need your help with this whole media blowout. We arrived at the gallery this morning and we couldn't even get in without security."

Shiori sighs delicately. "I knew it could go one or two ways. This could have been a onetime occurrence, and when they realized you weren't an easy target, they would move on. But I guess your display only made them more desperate to talk to you. I'm sorry it has come to this."

"Me too," I breathe.

"How can I help?" I had been afraid she'd be reluctant, or at least annoyed, but she seems more than willing to assist me.

"I'm not sure exactly, but Alex seems to think if you can draw the attention back to yourself, let the media know that you'll answer questions," I begin cautiously. "Maybe they'll leave me alone because I won't be necessary anymore."

Shi hums quietly while she thinks it over. "You must know I never have public press conferences, and I certainly never talk to the paparazzi."

I wince, hearing her bring my fears out in the open. "I know. That's why I was hesitant to call."

She continues to hum, and I can hear the click-clack of laptop keys on the other end of the line. "Let me talk to my

PR agent and see what I can do while still not appearing in person. That's a hard no for me, unfortunately. I don't want to set a precedent for making a statement about every little bit of excitement that goes on in my life. I think I have an idea, but I want to make sure it's worthwhile and will accomplish what we need it to."

Relief floods me, so much that tears prick at the corner of my eyes. There might be a way out of this, after all. "Thank you so—"

"Don't thank me yet," she interrupts, before sighing. "Sorry, I didn't mean to cut you off. I just don't want to disappoint you, is all."

A thought crosses my mind. "Shi... you don't think I'll mention this to Emma in a negative light if you can't help me, do you?"

She's silent on the other side of the call, which is all the answer that I need.

"I would never," I tell her in a whisper, trying to get my sincerity across. "Ever, Shiori. I know we don't know each other all that well, but I want you to be certain that I don't play those manipulative games. I won't even tell her I asked for your help if you don't want me to."

She remains quiet for a short time more, before letting out a huge breath. "It's rare to find people who aren't constantly playing games and trying to play everyone against each other for their own personal gain. I can't tell you how much of a relief it is to know you're not one of those people, but being Emma's best friend, I should've known." She gathers her composure before speaking again. "I'll do this task for you, not as a bargaining chip, but as a favor from one friend to another. Do you agree?"

I can't help but think how lucky Emma is. I had originally banked on Emma being attracted to Shiori's sharp mind and glossy, bright persona, but I'd have never guessed how warm her heart was. I recall her going toe to toe with Yara, and for a brief second, I think of Glinda the Good Witch and the Wicked Witch of the West from *Wizard of Oz* and fight back an absurd laugh. It has definitely been a long few days.

"I agree," I tell her. "A favor between friends."

"Perfect. Now, let me go wake up my PR agent and I'll get back to you once I have an answer." I'm about to hang up when she speaks up again. "And Petra? Emma messaged me asking about the best hotels in Tokyo..." Her tone is conspiratorial, as if we are high schoolers sharing secrets behind the bleachers at a football game.

I giggle. "She's hooked then."

"I hope so. I'll talk to you soon."

Bereft of anything else to do besides obsessively search up articles about my debacle yesterday, I decide to see how Alex and his security team are doing. Before I can open my office door, though, my phone rings. I'm surprised, and I can't help wondering why Shi would call back so quickly, but it's actually my dad calling. And somehow, I have a sinking feeling that this isn't a call to check in on me.

"Hi, Dad," I say as I answer.

"Hi, darling. Before anything else, are you okay? It's alarming how quickly Alex left yesterday, and the video I saw about you was distressing." He sounds exasperated, but some of my anxiety dissipates, knowing that he's just worried about me.

"We're handling it." I don't want to tell him I'm fine because, really, I've had better days. "Everything is under control."

Dad chuckles. "Well, I have no doubt of that. Alex is not one to take something like that sitting down. Which brings me to why I really called… where is my business partner? We were supposed to have a sit down with some important investors today, but I had to reschedule because he won't even answer my calls."

Ah, here we are. "He's busy, Dad."

"Busy micromanaging things that he could've employees do independently?" Dad guesses. I hate that he's right, because that is exactly what Alex is doing. What I don't say, though, is how happy I am that Alex is micromanaging. It makes me feel safer, and more confident, knowing he is just a staircase away.

"I'm not sure," I tell him. It isn't really a lie… it's not like I can see what Alex is doing right this second.

"You're as vague and forthcoming as always," Dad grumbles. "Do me a favor, darling daughter, tell your husband to please call me the hell back, because I'm certainly not his assistant to be moving his appointments around."

Ugh! Some things never change. "I'm not *your* assistant either, Dad. Nor am I your messenger."

"Just tell him for me, Petra." His annoyed tone of voice makes me think of how he would scold me as a child, and I really don't like recalling such memories.

"Fine," I snipe back. "Bye."

Dad's call managed to throw me right off of the high I had been on from my successful talk with Shiori, and I'm sure it seems like a rain cloud is hovering over my head when I find Alex in a quiet discussion with a few members of his security team and two police officers.

Nice for them to finally show up, I think sarcastically, but bite my tongue.

Alex turns, and I crook a finger at him, motioning him away from the gaggle of guards and officers so I can have a private word with him.

"How's it going?" I ask in a low voice.

"Hmm. Well enough. Despite having cameras already installed, we need to set up glass break and motion detectors as well as door contacts, but the biggest problem we're running into is with the windows. They're absolutely ancient, and the stained-glass ones are hopeless. They suggested changing them to a more resistant glass, but I'm sure you'd wring my neck if my team would do so."

"Don't you dare touch my stained glass!" I gasp, momentarily distracted from what I'd come to talk to him about.

He holds up his hands in a "slow down" motion. "Alright, alright, we'll only do glass break and motion detectors, then." He turns to look back at the men he had been talking to briefly, before his attention returns to me. "Do you need something? I was talking to the police about paying a little more attention to the gallery."

"Actually, yes. Can I see your phone?"

He looks bewildered, but hands it to me without preamble. It's immediately obvious he had silenced it, because as soon as I touch the screen, it lights up with notifications. I hold it up, pointing at the notification of eight missed calls from Roy.

"Love, I appreciate everything you're doing for me, but avoiding my dad just means he's going to bother me instead. Which he is… Can you just call him?"

Alex looks like he wants to argue, but he just gives me a curt nod, taking his phone back. "I'll wrap up this conversation and call him. I just knew he was going to blow up on me and I didn't want to waste my time."

"It isn't a waste of time to talk to your business partner, who is also your father-in-law, may I remind you," I tell him with a smirk creasing across my lips.

"Okay, okay, you've made your point. Did you call Shiori?"

"Yes," I answer proudly. "She's going to get back to me once she has an answer." I reach forward and link our fingers together in a quick gesture of affection. "You were right, though. She wasn't angry or bothered at all. How did you know?"

Alex smiles knowingly. "You don't see it yet, wife, but you're building a social circle of your very own, completely separate from the people your dad and I know. And this—" He reaches forward to tap the area over my heart. "Pure heart attracts the same. If you liked this Shiori, I knew she had to be a good person."

A thought flows through my mind, more like a vision. Everyone I've met, befriended and loved, all in one place. There's Emma, Matt, Sarah, Shiori, and other people I've only briefly met but felt a connection with. A shiver of what seems almost like prophecy races through me.

"Trust your judgment," Alex tells me, raising our interlocked fingers to his lips before letting go. "I don't think it's as likely to lead you astray as you think it is."

My vision fades from my mind, and I'm left with a feeling of excitement and joy for what's to come. "I'll try."

* * *

At 1 pm, Alex finally leaves for work, and I don't envy the conversation he's inevitably going to have with my dad. I'm sad to see him go, especially when there are still a decent throng of paparazzi outside, but I know he can't hold my hand all day.

From my side, I've given my statement to the police for the second time in two days, and while they seem pretty much unbothered, they promise to keep a better eye on the gallery during their patrols. They caution that as long as the paparazzi stay on the public sidewalks, there isn't much they can do unless they see them actively harassing someone. I'm more than perturbed at their words, but I tell them I understand. Manhattan is a big place, covered in glamor but with a dark and seedy underbelly. I'm sure these officers had imagined their careers would be kicking down doors for drug busts and arresting murderers, not escorting a timid art gallery owner every morning.

The only thing I enjoyed was watching Alex's security guards clash with the police. Alex had briefly introduced me to Pascal, the head of my brand-new security detail, and while he was barely taller than him, he seemed to love going toe to toe with the cocky police officers.

It's also clear that Pascal has been dying for a leadership position because he's jumped into the role with gusto, letting the officers know, in no uncertain terms, that he'll take no nonsense from any journalist or paparazzi. I had to cover my mouth when he told them he would "taze the balls off of anyone that came at my client." So, at least I'm in excellent hands there.

I have to give it to my husband, too. He may have royally pissed off my dad, but he hasn't wasted his time here at the gallery. Within an hour of him departing, an unmarked van arrives out front. It makes me nervous at first, watching the workers get out and start unloading gear from the back of the van, but Pascal is quick to let me know they are there to install the security measures that Alex had asked for. It must have cost a small fortune and taken some serious negotiating skills to get them out here on such short notice, but it's wonderful knowing that there would be no time wasted on properly securing my gallery. I could sleep easily tonight.

Of course, Alex had hired the best, and they didn't even turn their heads as the now thinned out crowd of journalists tried to ask them what they were here for. Once inside, I squander no time in letting them know I'll be observing all the installations, because everything in this building, down to the last brick, is worth something. Even the building is a piece of art, and I don't like the idea of anyone drilling holes into the antique stone or beautifully aged wooden windowsills.

I'm watching them install an impossibly small motion detector in the corner of Shiori's exhibit, when the artist herself calls me back. It's a FaceTime request, which surprises me, so I excuse myself to take it in my office.

When I answer, I can immediately see that Shiori is having makeup applied by someone, while someone else is combing a serum through her perfectly glossy, midnight hair. "Sorry for the video call. I can't exactly hold the phone up to my ear."

"No problem," I say slowly, taking it all in. "What's going on? Isn't it like, two am there?"

"Yes, but it doesn't matter since I'm going to be talking to predominantly American media," Shi clarifies, closing her eyes while her makeup artist expertly applies a sweep of eyeliner.

I lean forward in my chair, heart racing. "What do you mean?"

Shiori's smile is graceful and knowing. "My own PR team was able to contact a large majority of the outlets that have been bothering you. They have signed contracts that guarantee that they will leave you and your family alone, and in return, they'll have private press access to the online conference I am holding in forty-five minutes."

My jaw drops. "Shiori! That's amazing! I–I…" I stutter. "Can I thank you now?"

She laughs, and it reminds me of tinkling bells. "Yes, go ahead."

I thank her profusely. I don't fail to notice that in less than two months I have had two potential media problems, first in Aspen, and now here. When Margaret offered to help, it was at the enormously high price of breaking up Yara and Emma. When Shiori offered, though, she asked for nothing, and that fills my chest with a warm feeling.

Shiori takes my thanks gracefully but lets me know she only had little time to talk. Before we disconnect, I watch one of her makeup artists lower a jeweled, emerald-green half mask over her face. It only covers her eyes, but it gives me pause.

"You're still wearing masks even though you've revealed your face?" I ask, genuinely curious.

"Of course," Shiori says airily. "If there is anything that the public loves, it's a show. They love the mystique of it all. I have to keep them guessing, you know?"

I lean back in my chair, thinking about how much I still have to learn about manipulating the media to work in my favor. "Yeah, I know. Well, have a good conference. Call me if anything comes up."

CHAPTER 5

Manhattan, February 7, 2022
Petra

A few days have passed since Shi's press conference, and blessedly, her plan seems to have worked. The next morning, I had stopped by the gallery before heading to my classes, and there had been a scant five reporters milling around. The day after, just two. And today? Not a single reporter seems to be around.

Shi had sent me the whole video of the conference, where she had spoken, without naming names, about her exhibit in Tokyo and a potential new relationship, but warned her fans that if people continued to be harassed to find out bits and pieces of gossip about her, she'd go completely underground again and would make no further public appearances.

After taking a number of questions, Shiori had ended the digital press conference, but not before instructing the reporters to go through her PR agency for questions rather than trying to speak to anyone else about it. That had seemed to fix the issue for the most part, and I was happy to pretend the chaotic few days had just been an anomaly.

Alex hasn't budged on the security issue, though, and even now that I'm studying in the library, I know one of Alex's guards is somewhere not too far so they can monitor me. I have to admit, I don't love having someone shadowing my every step, but in an effort to keep the peace, I've sucked it up and allowed it for now.

One of the best parts about being able to continue living my normal life is the reunion of my study group. After spending so much time with older, established adults all the time, getting to hang out with people my own age feels like a breath of fresh air. Of course, being able to study for my courses is a boon too.

Getting together today in Columbia's library feels just like my freshman year again, back when everything was so much less complicated. Matt and Sarah are sitting on one side of the long table, close enough that their legs touch, and I'm on the other side, next to David and Kate. We talk in low voices, comparing notes and filling in the blanks for parts we had missed or hadn't understood from lectures. It's always a shock to see how different everyone's notes for the same class are, but seeing it through someone else's eyes make some of the more difficult ideas easier to understand.

I appreciate that I'm still invited, even though I'm taking fewer classes this year than everyone else. Thankfully, everyone has been treating me the same too regardless of the fact that I'm now a wife and a mother. It's such a departure from the conspiratorial, underhanded world I had immersed myself in lately that it makes my head spin, but in a good way.

"I miss winter break already," Matt grumbles, tapping his pencil on the worn wooden tabletop. His class load is three times the size of mine, and I get the feeling that Matt is ready to graduate at the earliest opportunity.

"Matt, just stick to YouTube, I'm sure you'll have more success in that than in becoming a prof," David replies, laughing under his breath.

Matt scowls, crumples a piece of paper in his hand, and launches it at David.

"Knock it off!" Sarah hisses, slapping Matt's arm. "How old are you exactly?"

I hide my laugh behind my hands, trying to keep the volume down before we catch anyone's attention. The other two girls roll their eyes, burying their attention back in their notes while the boys continue to glare and make faces at each other. I try to imagine Alex behaving like this, when he was younger and carefree, and the thought of it makes me smile.

I've been at school for the majority of the day, so when a text pops up on my phone, I assume it's from my husband asking if I'll be home for dinner. Instead, it's from Emma, and I take a deep, calming breath before opening it. If she was going to meet Shi in Tokyo, Emma would have left last Friday, but so far, she hasn't mentioned anything to me. I've pushed it to the back of my mind, refusing to believe that Emma would squander this chance., I'll get proof from either her or Shi sooner or later.

Now that I have my potential proof in my hands, though, I feel reluctant. But I have to know! Slowly, I turn my phone over, flicking past the home screen to Emma's message. To my biggest surprise, it's a picture, and thank goodness, my friend still had enough sense in her head to make the right choice.

The shot is of her and Shi at Shi's exhibit in Tokyo, both of them dressed impeccably and smiling, as if they weren't the center of attention for the entire city. I gasp from excitement, earning looks of suspicion not just from my friend group, but some of the other tables around us.

Emma's text read:

I wasn't sure if I was actually going to go until I was boarding the plane! I was so nervous, but you were right. I'm so happy to be here. Thank you, babe. <3

I hold the phone close to my chest, ecstatic. If I wasn't in a university library, I would jump out of my chair and do a little victory dance. I've done it! I can't believe I've beaten Yara and helped Emma realize what she really wanted out of a partner. To top it all off, I wasn't telling Margaret half-truths anymore either. Emma and Shi are well on their way to being a legit couple.

Mostly, though, I'm happy to have something that will piss off Yara, and there's nothing she can do about it. That will show her to underestimate me.

I know I'm weirding out my study partners, but I don't care. I want to savor this moment. I decide to forward the picture and send it to Catherine. She's an unlikely hero for me, but she had really come through on this one. Her having tickets to Shiori's auction was a one in a million chance, but somehow the older woman had known her setup was going to work.

Catherine texts back after a few minutes, and I ignore the raised eyebrows of the rest of the table that I'm texting *again* during the study group.

What an achievement! Well done! Can I invite you out for a glass to celebrate? I have a few other things I'd like to discuss with you if you have time.

According to the time on my phone, I still have two hours until our study session would officially be over, and Alex would expect me home. Since I have fewer classes than everyone else, I don't have much more to study for today... Screw it, I deserve to celebrate my achievement, like Catherine said! I message Pascal to let him know we are leaving and break the news to the rest of the group that I'm finished for the day. There are frowns all around, and I'm sure that they're annoyed that I won't tell them why I'm leaving or why I was so distracted. Oh well. They'd see it on the news soon enough, I'm sure.

I gather my things and give everyone a quick goodbye. I promise them I will be there for the whole time next week, and I assume they think I've got something going on with the babies, so they don't ask too many questions, even though I can see that they are all curious.

I'm at the grand salon at the Baccarat hotel next to the MoMA, Catherine tells me once I reach the car, and I give the location to the driver, sitting back to relax.

I wonder what she would want to talk to me about? As far as I know, nothing is going on between Dad and Catherine, and to my pleasant surprise, Catherine had yet to try and wheedle any information out of me regarding my dad's business life. I'm willing to consider that I might have judged her too harshly when I first met her, but only time would tell.

The plush, platinum and champagne-hued grand salon is welcoming, bright, and clearly high class, with gleaming chandeliers hanging from its high ceiling and a soft jazz music playing in the background. Catherine is sitting at one of the low tables, her legs daintily crossed, enjoying an afternoon tea accompanied by cupcakes and a flute of champagne. She's wearing a beige sheath dress and matching pumps, showing off her impressively long legs. I feel underdressed in my sweater, All Stars, and comfortable jeans, but then I realize Catherine is probably dressed up all the freaking time.

"Petra," Catherine all but purrs, pulling me in for a European style kiss on both cheeks. "So lovely to see you. What will you be having?"

I rarely drink, but since this is a celebration, after all… "Champagne, please."

The bartender brings me a glass over after Catherine waves him down, and it's deliciously dry and bubbly on my tongue.

"I'm so glad everything worked out for your friend," Catherine says, a pleasant smile gracing her lips. "I thought Shiori might have been a long-shot, but it seems they fell for each other rather quickly."

"Yes, you're right. Honestly, the best I was hoping for was a fling that would knock some sense into Emma, but I think this might be something *real* between them. Who could have guessed?"

"Everyone loves a happy ending," Catherine says, smiling behind her glass of champagne before taking a sip.

We talk about everything that had happened since the art auction—at least everything I was comfortable telling her—and she listens as if riveted. I'm well aware that Catherine has the potential to repeat all of my gossip back to Margaret, so she gets the very abbreviated version of events.

We're on our second glass when Catherine's phone rings. As she looks at the screen, her expression remains totally neutral and instead of excusing herself to take the call in private, she answers right there at the table. I know I shouldn't, but I listen carefully. After all, she hadn't felt the need to walk away.

"Julia!" Catherine exclaims. "So nice to hear your voice, darling. How have you been?"

I freeze, carefully setting my glass down on the glass table. *Julia's a common name...* I try to assure myself. Surely I wouldn't be unlucky enough to be sitting in on a call between Julia Van Den Bosch and Catherine? Alex has spoken to Julia recently, as he had told me, but we haven't talked about her since.

But, of course, it's me and my fantastically bad luck. It hits me that there is no way it's anyone *but* Alex's sister Julia. After all, it's Julia's friendship with Catherine that brought her into our social circle to begin with. I sit stiffly, glancing around the decoration of the salon while Catherine asks about Sebastian and the kids, and the two women embark in a round small talk. Unfortunately, I can only hear Catherine's side of the conversation.

For a second, I wonder if the whole "meet up for drinks" thing was just a setup, but the way Catherine talks to Julia, with genuine, warm affection in her voice, makes me think otherwise. Either she's a phenomenal actress, which is possible, or this really is just a case of bad luck.

"Oh, me? I'm just sitting here having a drink with Petra. Yes, silly, that Petra. Hm? Well, let me ask her." Catherine lays her hand over her phone and turns to me, not an ounce of apology in her expression. She must not know how much I *don't* want to talk to Julia until I cringe, taking the phone. Catherine mouths, "Sorry!" to me, but otherwise seems unbothered, picking up her glass to drink again.

"Hi, Julia," I say, trying to keep my tone as neutral as possible.

"Petra!" she exclaims. "So nice to hear from you. I'm surprised to hear that you're spending time with Catherine, but glad about it. She needs friends in Manhattan, surely."

I do my best to keep a poker face, but Julia's bubbly tone is already gritting on my nerves. "Yes, we've been getting on quite well."

"Wow, how long has it been since we've spoken? Since Jasmine and Jasper's baptism, right?" Julia asks, her voice always so sweet and friendly, just like the first time we met. I pinch the bridge of my nose, trying to fight off a headache. It's just a phone conversation. All I need to do is make some polite small talk and then find a reason to get off the line.

"I think you're correct. How have you been?"

We launch into inane chit chat, all fluff and no substance. This is the only type of safe conversation with most of Alex's family. Julia keeps trying to press me with personal questions, but I manage to keep her from digging too deep into my life.

"Did Alex tell you I called?" she asks finally.

"Yes. I was in St. Moritz actually–" I catch myself and clamp my mouth shut. Talking about St. Moritz meant talking about Yara, and as far as I know, only me and Margaret know about Emma.

"I know," Julia says nonchalantly. "It seems like you managed to solve that minor problem effectively. Well done," she praises.

I'm taken aback, and it takes me a moment to answer. "Oh, you knew?" I ask, trying to keep my voice even so she doesn't hear my shock.

"Of course!" she answers like it was obvious. "I'm actually surprised you were so efficient. Your friend Emma seemed very much in love with my sister. Although," Julia begins, "Yara is a hard one to love, including for herself, even, it seems. Hopefully, now that you've worked your magic, she'll settle down with Elliot and stop stepping out."

I think about the masquerade in Venice and everything Alex told me about her. *Not likely*, I think, but instead I say, "Well, I had little choice in the matter."

"Indeed," she drawls. "I don't know the minute details, but I get the impression that Mother had a heavy hand when convincing you. But maybe you've discovered a new talent! Matchmaking!"

Yuck! "Actually, I think I've had enough matchmaking for the rest of my life."

"Oh, nonsense. We must pursue what talents the universe graces us with, you know?" I don't answer, glad she couldn't see me rolling my eyes. Catherine, sitting next to me, seems to suppress a laugh.

Julia doesn't seem to be deterred by my awkward silence, though. She has an agenda, so she pushes on. "Since you were so talented at finding a new flame for your friend, there's someone else that needs your help."

"What?" I utter, barely believing it. Who else could this family seriously want me to fix up? I'm so done with them! Done! "I'm not interested in repeating the experience," I say firmly. "It was not an enjoyable time for me, and it took way too much time out of my life."

"But you succeeded, lil sister. Brilliantly too. Emma and Shiori are a stunning couple, you must admit."

"I know," I huff. "I hooked them up, remember?"

Julia makes a noise of displeasure. "There's no reason to be sarcastic. I'm not asking you for anything extraordinary."

I bristle at her comment, but I bite my tongue. An argument will mean we have to talk on the phone even longer. "Julia, I have children to care for, a business to manage, and I'm still going to school. I don't have time to be a matchmaker."

She blows out a breath, and when she speaks again, she has evened out her voice and seems to be on the verge of pleading with me. "If you help me out, Petra, I promise you that Yara will never bother you ever again."

"Why would she bother me? It's not like bullying me will make Emma want to take her back."

"Come on. You know Yara, she isn't exactly reasonable. She seemed rather displeased with your little setup. Not sure what she's got in mind, but knowing my sister as I do, it's better to be careful."

I heave a long sigh, already regretting having accepted to speak with her in the first place. Yet I can't forget Yara's threat when I was about to embark the plane. That woman is batshit crazy. And yeah, God knows what she's capable of, especially now that Emma is with Shi in Tokyo. "If I help you out," I begin cautiously, "not only does Yara leave me alone, but you, your mom, and everyone else too."

"I promise, dear. We'll never bother you ever again." Julia sounds almost giddy.

I close my eyes in exasperation. I hate this. I hate talking to Julia, I hated that she seemed to think that I was beholden to her, or that I had to do something for her in order for her to help me with Yara. If we were sisters like she just said, wouldn't she help me because she cared about me? Like Shiori had just days ago?

But there is nothing to be done, and I know it. If there is anything that Alex's family is good at, it's being master manipulators, and Julia managed to back me into a corner over a ten-minute spontaneous phone conversation, all the while never becoming angry or nasty like Yara would have. She seems as perfectly controlled and reasonable as ever, but she's given me no choice. The temptation of having Yara and Margaret out of my hair forever, with Julia to back me up, is too strong.

"Alright," I sigh, defeated. "What can I do for you?"

"Oh Petra, I'm so excited that you're going to help. I just know you'll be the perfect person for the job, and this means

I can keep it in the family without it leaking into the rumor mill."

"Sure," I mutter, unable to match her excitement. "But you still haven't said what you need."

"It's easy, actually. I just need you to find the perfect woman for a young, helpless romantic."

It sounds suspect. Maybe too easy. "For whom, exactly?"

She takes a deep breath, as if she's about to reveal some tremendous secret. "My son."

"Which one?" I blurt out, startled. I really didn't see this coming. Did Julia really trust me to find someone for one of her precious sons? I shift in my seat, my curiosity sparked.

"My oldest, Andries. He needs someone serious. Someone who is good for him."

"Nonsense, Julia," I rebuke. "Andries is my age. I'm settled down, sure, but most people my age aren't and don't want to be. Just let him date around and find someone himself. Be patient."

"You don't understand," she insists. "He's very much in love with a lady but she's... not right for him."

"How can you even know that?" I ask, incredulous. "If he loves her, then she's right for him, isn't she? Don't you trust his judgment?"

"Not when it comes to this." She exhales heavily, as if she's already thought over this situation dozens of times. "Trust me, I know."

"I need more details than that," I tell her, trying to keep my tone even, though it's getting harder at every passing second. "I barely know him, and I need to know why you assume that his chosen partner is so completely wrong for him."

"It's a long story. A really, really long story. I'd rather talk about the details personally." She says it so blithely that I almost don't realize what she just suggested. When it hits me, I'm immediately angry.

"I'm not going to the Netherlands!" I snap straight away. "I just came from Europe."

For the first time during this conversation, I hear a thread of the same ruthlessness I've heard in Yara's and Margaret's voices before. "Oh, don't worry, my brother is coming too."

"What?" I'm nearly gasping for air. Alex told me he had declined her invitation. Then I remember how he railroaded me into going to Aspen, and I have a sinking feeling that he did it once more. "He told me the opposite. Did you speak to him again?"

"Sebastian did," Julia tells me smugly. "After all, it's his birthday in twelve days, so he invited my brother himself."

If it had been my cell phone and not Catherine's, I'd have launched it across the room. I have escalated from angry to royally pissed off. After everything they did to us, I can't believe Alex had the audacity to accept Sebastian's invitation without even consulting me! I know they were very close when growing up, but still. Or else Julia is bluffing. But I have a sneaking suspicion that she's telling me the truth. It had been the trump card she was hiding up her sleeve.

Since I can't throw the cell phone to the floor, I just grit my teeth and tell Julia, "I really, really don't like you right now."

Julia's laugh is slightly self-deprecating. "I'm sorry to hear that, but I think it's a good idea to meet up if we all want to turn the page."

Well, I don't. Despite her diplomatic tone, I don't have what it takes to match it. "I guess I'll go talk to my husband. I wish I could say it's been a pleasure Julia, but it hasn't."

"You're still so young and naive." She chuckles. "I understand you're still hurt, but I hope one day you'll move on."

"Goodbye," I say in return, right before I hang up.

I simply set Catherine's phone on the low table and leave the couch, going to the restroom to splash cold water on my face.

"Are you alright?" I hear Catherine asking as I leave the table behind me. "Do you want another drink?"

But I'm already too far away from her to reply.

Alone in the silent bathroom, my hair hangs down around my face as I catch my breath, frigid water pebbling on my skin and running off while I examine my reflection. I still look like myself—healthy, youthful, and beautiful... so why do I feel so drained? I'm honestly so over being used. Just this afternoon, I was enjoying being a normal college student. Now I'm right back in the last place I wanted to be.

When I come back to the table, I notice a fresh glass of champagne on my side. I had planned to leave immediately, but I'm just too angry and annoyed at Alex right now. I need some time to decompress. I sit back down on the sofa immediately bringing the champagne to my lips.

"I guess I should apologize, but I swear I had no idea what she was going to ask you," Catherine says, filling the strange silence between us.

"I believe you." I sip again. "Well, I want to believe you. I'll try, at least."

She nods. "We don't know each other all that well, so I'll take whatever trust you want to give me."

We finish up our drinks, any camaraderie built between us having fallen to the wayside. I'm almost regretting coming at all, but eventually I'd have to get to know my father's girlfriend if they were going to be serious. I excuse myself once my glass is empty, and Catherine doesn't argue. She embraces me quickly before I leave, but I respond with a lukewarm hug, ready to be alone.

Pascal is my driver tonight, taking over for Zach, who didn't have the careful training my head of security did. I notice he keeps glancing at me in the rearview mirror, a wrinkle of concern between his dark-brown eyes.

"Are you okay, ma'am?" he asks, sounding uncomfortable.

"Yes, thanks for asking. Just a lot on my mind," I admit.

"Understandable. You have a lot on your plate. Maybe a vacation is in order?"

I laugh bitterly. "You know what? All of my vacations lately have seemed like work so much more than being home and actually working. They're exhausting."

Pascal shrugs, tapping his fingers on the steering wheel. "Sounds like you need to go alone next time, then."

"That's a lovely idea," I say wistfully. I sink back into my seat, thinking about our honeymoon in North Island—crystal clear water and sugary white beach sand, with not a single thing around. I can almost feel the tropical sun on my skin, even as the real sun outside is completely obscured by dingy winter clouds.

I should be thinking about how I'm going to confront Alex, and what I'm going to do if he really insists we go to the Netherlands. We're going to fight, I just know it, and I don't want to even consider it at the moment. So for now, I ignore my problems, the three glasses of champagne making me feel flush and languid, fantasizing about the beach and endless days of no stress.

I usually love winter, but right now I'm utterly sick of snow, and rain, and cold, and the ever-present grayness of the city. I want to be anywhere else, but it's just a fantasy. Instead, I'll go home and ask my husband why we're going to a party I knew nothing about, and then do some homework.

But this summer break... I'm absolutely going to the beach.

CHAPTER 6

Petra

"Why aren't you eating?"

I look up at Alex, surprised, only to realize that he's right. I've just been pushing my dinner around my plate, lost in thought. Maria prepared a simple olive oil and garlic pasta, but my stomach has been in knots ever since I got home.

My talk with Julia stands as the elephant in the room, even if I'm not sure if Alex knows it's there. I'm amazed that he is able to just sit there and eat, making conversation with Jasmine held in his lap as if he hadn't betrayed me yet again by making promises about us going to the Netherlands. I want to give him the benefit of the doubt and try to believe that he's going to bring it up after the kids are in bed, but it's hard. Julia had made it sound like it was a definite thing—one that Alex clearly didn't feel the need to consult with me before agreeing.

There was another thought I had on the drive home, too. Alex has my dad, but what other friends does he have around here? Emma and Matt are the godparents to our children, but they are my friends, not really his.

Maybe that's why he was so eager to tell Sebastian that we would go to the Netherlands. He missed his friends, and he had already told me about how much the guilt of not seeing his nephews and nieces grow up was weighing on him. As I watch him cut noodles into tiny pieces for our daughter to pick up with her fat little hands, there's a pang in my heart. Being a father has probably made him miss them even more.

It's going to cause an argument between the two of us. Unless he agrees with me to stay here, it's inevitable. But I swear to myself that I'll be respectful toward him regardless of how things go down. Respectful and understanding, and I'll give him time to bring it up on his own without an ambush. He deserves that much.

"Petra?" Alex asks again.

I lay my hand over my stomach, waving a hand dismissively. "Sorry. I stopped by the Baccarat to gloat about my success with Catherine and I don't think the champagne is sitting well with me. It's been so long since I've drank."

Alex seems to buy it. "Well, even more reason for you to eat. It'll soak up all the alcohol in your stomach. Maybe some bread to go with it?"

"Maybe," I agree, plucking a piece of crusty bread from the center of the table. "Thank you, love."

I force myself to eat as if nothing is bothering me. After all, if I'm going to give Alex the opportunity to start the conversation, then I shouldn't tear myself up over it either. It'd happen in its own time.

Once the meal is over, I feel more centered, if a bit sleepy, and I go through the motions of bathing the kids for bed while yawning behind my hand often. This time of year has so few hours of daylight that my sleep schedule always seems to get messed up, and I know it will get worse the closer I get to finals.

Jasper is so peaceful in the bath, that getting him ready for bed is a breeze. He loves to clap the bubbles from the lavender-scented soap between his hands and squeeze the water from the washcloth. He mumbles and babbles to himself until his eyelids get heavy and we swap him out for his sister.

She doesn't enjoy bath time quite as much, wriggling like a salmon in my grasp, complaining in squeals and her nonsense baby language until the warmth of the water relaxes her at last. It doesn't bother me that she protests so many things, oddly enough. Jasmine's extremely opinionated, even without being able to talk, and I love to see the fire in her at this early age.

Even more, I love her little potbelly and the rolls on her legs and arms. She's still a petite baby, but it's so wonderful to see her putting on weight at pretty much the same rate as her brother. Jasmine is our little chunky miracle baby, and while I'm well aware that there are more struggles with her health likely in our future, so far everything has been going even better than we could have hoped.

I wrap her in a soft, fluffy towel and hand her off to Alex so I can wash my own face for the evening. I've piled my hair on top of my head and just finished removing my makeup in front of the sink when I feel eyes on me. I turn, and Alex is leaning against the door frame of the bathroom, his arms crossed and his gaze affectionate.

"You're beautiful," he tells me.

"Oh, hush." I laugh.

"So, beautiful wife, do you want to talk?"

Oh. I guess we're doing this now. "About what?" I ask as I apply my moisturizer.

"At dinner you mentioned you had been at the bar with Catherine. That, combined with your melancholy demeanor, started to make sense, so I messaged my sister to confirm. You talked to Julia, didn't you?"

I sigh, shoulders sagging. I remind myself I don't have any reason to feel guilty. "Yes, unwillingly."

"Okay. If I know Julia, she was probably gushing about our visit as her way of springing the news on you and then acting innocent. Am I right?" Alex's voice is even but I can tell that he's on edge, waiting to see how I would respond.

"Actually, no. She asked me for a favor and then dropped the bomb that Sebastian managed to change your mind about going to his party."

This makes him stand up a little bit straighter, confusion in his expression. "What favor could she possibly want from you?"

I shrug defeatedly, walking past Alex out into our bedroom to sit on the edge of the bed. I pat the space next to me, inviting him to sit down too, but he doesn't budge, staying in the doorway of the bathroom.

"Something about finding a girlfriend for her oldest son, Andries, because he's in love with some inappropriate woman. It seems your family is getting the idea that I'm ready and willing to find love for everyone," I say, wrinkling my nose.

Alex's expression clears, understanding coming over his features. "Ah, okay. Then her and Sebastian's stories line up. At least they weren't lying to us, like I half suspected they were."

It's my turn to be bewildered. "I was under the impression Sebastian simply invited you to his birthday party and that this love match ordeal was all Julia's idea."

"Andries pining over a woman is true," he declares, his tone heavier than usual. "Sebastian mentioned the same thing, but he made it seem a lot more serious." He heaves an exasperated breath, before adding, "Which is why I accepted his invitation."

I lean forward, desperate to put the pieces of this mystery together. Were Julia and Sebastian working together to try and manipulate Alex and I, or was it really just two worried parents reaching out for help with their son?

"More serious? How so?" I ask, intrigued on how this could possibly play out.

"Sebastian said since the breakup, his son has been staying locked in his room, all day and all night, only occasionally eating and basically shutting out the entire world." Alex sounds distressed, and he finally comes to sit next to me as he continues the story. "He told me there's a history of depression that runs in his family, and—" He purses his mouth, and with a start, I realize whatever he's trying to tell me is significant enough that it's difficult for him to say.

"It's okay," I murmur, rubbing my hand up and down his leg for comfort.

"Sebastian had a half-brother who committed suicide. He was Andries's age, and although he didn't say it so plainly, I can tell the memory is still haunting him."

I gasp, shocked. I was sure I was past the point of ever feeling sympathy toward anyone in Alex's family, but this hits me like a ton of bricks. While I hate Sebastian and Julia, I can relate with that fear of the unimaginable pain of losing their child.

"Andries has refused therapists, and Julia tried to have him go to a healing retreat to work on his mental health, but he refused that too. I know he's a grown man but Petra...." Alex swallows. "He's still my nephew, and he's only nineteen. I held him the day he was born, watched him blow out his birthday candles year after year... I love him. I love all the kids, and if I don't do what I can do to help, how can I live with myself?"

I scoot close to him, wrapping my arms around his body and letting him lean his weight into my body. He's so much heavier than I am, but I don't mind.

I don't answer his question right away, letting it hang in the air. Despite everything that Alex has said, I'm still not sure that we should go. Of course I wanted to help this poor Andries if I could, but how was seeing his uncle Alex and me, whom he had barely met, supposed to snap him out of whatever fugue he was in? I get that it might be a last-ditch effort by Sebastian and Julia, but I still have a hard time seeing the sense in it.

"I don't want to go, Alex," I say finally. "If you feel like you don't have any choice except to go, I won't stop you, but I'm tired of being manipulated by your family. I'm a complete stranger to Andries; he isn't going to care if I'm there or not."

"Sebastian seems to think the two of you might become friends," he discloses, his tone even. "There isn't anyone else his age in the family, and he might feel isolated."

"Julia said something similar, but…" I consider my words carefully. "I don't want us to be close to these people. I don't want to repair the relationship, and I certainly don't want to go to a birthday party in the Netherlands. If you feel like you have to go for your nephew, I will deal with it, but I'm not going."

Alex stiffens and pulls out of my embrace. "You said you were open to repair our relationship with them," he reminds me.

Crap! I do recall telling him that when I came back from my trip to St. Moritz. "Yes, but I never thought it'd be to go to this party!" I refute just as fast. "I told you that you had done well in declining the invitation."

His eyes widen and a scowl forms on his face. "Yes, but back then I didn't know what was going on with my nephew." He sounds irritated and maybe even hurt I'm not going along with his plan, but I look him straight in the eye, holding my ground.

"I'm not going," I tell him once more, my decision made. "If you want to go, then go by yourself."

His brows are furrowed with confusion, as if trying to figure something out. "So you don't give a shit, huh?"

"That's not fair," I respond, stung. "Of course I do, but Andries is a stranger to me, and I can't help but think you're letting yourself be twisted into the same old patterns with them, too."

"They're my family, Petra," he says bluntly. "We might be estranged most of the time, but nothing will ever change that there's a bond between all of us."

"Not even the death of my mother?" I blurt out, slapping my hands over my traitorous mouth as soon as I say it. I wish I could take my words back immediately.

Alex shoots to his feet, almost vibrating with anger. "It finally comes out, then! That's how you really feel?"

"I can't help it," I gulp through the lump in my throat. "She was my mom, Alex, and parts of your family had a hand in her death. No matter what she did to me, I can't just forget what they have done."

"But this is about my nephew! Not Julia or Sebastian!" Alex paces the floor, his hands clenched in fists at his side. I just watch, all of my previous righteous indignation having bled out of me the minute this discussion crossed the line into full blown fight. Still, though, what I said was the truth.

Alex stops, seeming to have come to some sort of conclusion. "I know you're hurt, but we need to help him out. Plus, it'll be good for the kids to be surrounded by other children. We can leave right after the party, but we're going." His tone is neither stern, nor harsh, but his words, even if delivered with soft gloves, are enough to make me jump up in rage.

"Oh hell no!" I shout in response, before snatching my phone off the charger and fleeing up the stairs to my atelier. I couldn't stay in that bedroom a second longer, being suffocated by the tension in the room and Alex's shameful demand.

I slam the atelier door behind me, pressing my back against it and sliding to the floor. I wrap my arms around my knees, lower my head, and take some heavy breaths in frustration, a few tears coursing silently down my cheeks. Of course I'm hurt! They killed my mother, for fuck's sake! And yet, here they are, always trying to win us over. It feels like this will never end.

* * *

After what has to be an hour or so of angry painting, and a cup of chamomile tea which was brought up by a nervous-looking Maria, I've calmed down enough to think straight. I look at the small canvas in front of me, now covered with a stark scene of black trees against snow, and think about what my next steps with my family should be.

Alex owes me one hell of an apology to have decided to attend that party without even consulting me. I might have invited them to the baptism, but that was the last time I wanted to see them. Now I can't stop thinking about Mom and what they did to her. We hadn't had a perfect relationship by any means, but she was still my mom. And I've still had to raise my children without her help and influence.

I'd never wish anything bad on Alex's family, but the fact of the matter is, they are all alive and thriving. Even if his contact with them had been minimized, he's still in a better position than me.

His heart is still whole. But I'm not sure if mine is.

On the other hand, I know how it feels to not be with your family, and to have those relationships stretched so thin they might snap. If I can spare Alex those feelings, and maybe let my kids have a relationship with some of Alex's more normal family members like his nieces and nephews, I should probably pursue it.

No! It isn't fair.

It'll never be fair that Margaret gets to live her life to the fullest, getting to see Jasmine and Jasper grow, while my own mother never will. She never even got to meet them.

I shake my head, trying to banish all of these thoughts. They won't help anything, and they certainly won't do any good with fixing the problem I've found myself dealing with. The only thing this line of thinking can do is upset me.

I need to think, and behave, logically. Before I can think any more about my mother, I force myself to make a plan to tackle everything. It really seems like it might be a coincidence that Sebastian talked to Alex so recently, just like I had Julia, but I needed to be sure it wasn't some carefully built plan intended to back me into a corner. If it turns out that everyone had plotted against me, then I was going to fight tooth and nail to not go to this birthday.

I tap my paintbrush on the easel as I think. I had already asked Catherine if our drink date had been a setup, and she had told me no. And I really do want to believe her, but I just don't know if I can. I do know I have to get to the bottom of this, though, or I'll never be able to rest.

After considering it for a few long moments, I finally decide to call Catherine. She surely interacts with Julia more than Alex does, so if anyone knows the truth, it's her. I'm hoping against hope that she doesn't have anything to do with this potential setup, but I'm not holding my breath.

She picks up on the second ring, sounding slightly wary that I'm contacting her so soon after just having seen her at the bar. "Hello?"

"Hey, Catherine. So, the whole talk I had with Julia? I guess Sebastian called Alex too, and Alex is under the impression that we're going to Sebastian's birthday."

She doesn't reply, but I let the comment hang in the air, giving her some time to think about it. When I realize that she isn't going to respond, I continue on my own. "I know I already asked, but—"

"No, I did not set you up so Julia could talk to you. I obviously have no way to prove that fact to you, but do you really think I'd risk your father's ire just so my friend could have a phone call with her own sister-in-law? Had I realized the issues between you two, I'd have never mentioned your presence."

"Okay," I say simply. I'm apparently never going to know the full truth of it, and I'm not sure if I'm happy or annoyed that Catherine is sticking to her original story. I really do want to believe her.

"I do have to tell you something, though, because I know if you find out on your own you're going to be convinced of my guilt."

This gives me pause. "What do you need to tell me?"

Catherine sighs daintily, as if having to divulge all this information is leaving a bad taste in her mouth. "Your father and I will be at the party too. We were invited ages ago."

I stutter for a second, at a loss for words. If Alex planning to go see Julia and Sebastian had felt like betrayal to me, it was nothing compared to knowing that my own dad had plans to go to Sebastian's party. Heck, he isn't even close with anyone that would be there, and I'm left flabbergasted trying to wrap my mind around why he would willingly hang out with the family that killed his ex-wife.

"Why didn't you tell me at the bar?" I ask, a note of hysteria in my voice.

"I was assuming that your father would tell you himself, but when I mentioned it to him, he seemed to just brush the issue off. I'm not sure if he knows how upset you would be, so he put off telling you for that reason, or if he really is being dismissive of the whole situation. I don't want there to be a big, dramatic blow out at the birthday party, which is why I'm telling you now." Catherine pauses, thinking over her next words. "That, and it wouldn't be fair for you to come to the party and see us there. It'd be quite the shock, I'm sure."

If Catherine is being honest, then I actually do appreciate her spilling the beans since Dad didn't bother to do so himself. When I really think about it, his attitude toward the whole thing is very reminiscent of my childhood. Choosing not to tell me things that would be important for me to know simply because he didn't want to deal with my emotional fallout from it.

Some things never change, I guess.

"Thank you, Catherine." I don't know what else to say, but I do know I want to talk to my dad desperately.

"Well, I'm sure you've gathered that Roy and I are going because I am close friends with Julia, so in a way, I'm responsible. The only right thing to do was inform you."

After I'm finished talking to Catherine, I ponder the idea of painting something else before I call Dad so I can get my thoughts together. Eventually, though, I decide I need to just confront him. The quicker I lance the wound of him going behind my back, the easier I would rest tonight.

My mind's racing, so I load up another miniature canvas on the easel, planning to just paint a quick and messy daytime version of the painting I had done earlier. Maybe my nerves will be calmer if I'm distracted during the conversation.

To my total astonishment, when I'm grabbing a few tubes of paint, Dad calls me instead. I sit on my art stool and answer. Dad doesn't sound bothered, or like he is dreading the conversation we're about to have. Instead, he asks me the usual questions about Jasmine and Jasper, school, and the gallery. He listens intently, fully engaged as if he really is just checking up on me.

Strangely, the inane chit chat is making me even more nervous. I feel like we are both just avoiding the inevitable confrontation, so in the middle of Dad telling me about a company golf trip he is considering planning, I interrupt ready to have everything out in the open.

"Dad," I say stiffly. "You and Catherine are going to Sebastian's birthday party, aren't you?"

Dad sighs raggedly. "Damn Catherine. I told her I'd tell you in my own time. But yes, I'm going to the Netherlands to check on our local office and accepted the invitation. Catherine wouldn't miss it for the world."

"But Dad, after everything they've done to us, how can you just want to make friends and play nice? Just send Catherine alone! You don't have to deal with all of that!"

He coughs, trying to fill the silence. "Actually, she had agreed to go alone, but I offered to go as a couple."

I feel like my blood instantly turns to ice in my veins. I had been hoping, up until this point, that Dad was just getting dragged along unwillingly, but knowing that it was *his* idea is hurtful in a completely different way, and as much as I have tried to push those thoughts away, they still come back, unbidden.

"They killed Mom!" I blurt out, tears in my voice. "They killed your ex-wife, and you're going to go hang out with them like it's no big deal? How can you do that?"

Dad curses under his breath, before taking a huge breath. "Life goes on, Petra. Your grudges can't be mine, just like I'd never expect mine to be yours."

"Life goes on?" I snort, totally left flabbergasted. "Life goes on for who?" I repeat, my voice higher. "Not me, I'll tell you that! I haven't forgotten the things they did, like so many other people. And I don't forgive them, either!"

"Catherine is my partner, and Sebastian and Julia are Catherine's friends. I love you, Petra, but you can't expect everyone to stand around in the past just because you want to."

Holy shit. His comment is as cold as ice, and totally devoid of any emotion. "Well, at least Catherine had the nerve to be honest with me."

Dad huffs in indignation. "I was going to tell you. She just jumped the gun and did it before I was ready."

"Whatever." I'm gripping my paintbrush so hard I'm surprised it hasn't broken yet. "Everyone in my life is just going to do whatever the hell they want with no concern for my feelings or Mom's memory. I hope you guys have a great time."

"Petra, honey–"

I hang up the phone, powering it down before clasping my hands behind my head and leaning forward on the stool, trying to maintain my composure and not lose control again. I breathe deeply, in and out, until the adrenaline that had flushed my system fades away, leaving me calmer but absolutely exhausted.

I decide to finish my little daytime forest painting, laying it out to dry with its twin. Seeing how I'm able to channel all my negative emotions makes me feel a little bit better, but not enough to matter. This Netherlands trip is breathing down the back of my neck. Everyone is closing in on me at all sides, and I have no idea who to turn to, or what to do.

The idea of bringing a pillow and blanket to the atelier and sleeping up here is tempting, just to show Alex how serious I am about not going to Sebastian's party. We never sleep apart, so I'm sure he would notice right away, but as I look around the studio, I realize sleeping on the floor isn't going to be very comfortable. I guess I could always sleep in one of the guest bedrooms. Decided, I dial Maria's phone number and ask her to get it ready for me. "And don't forget to bring my pajamas and toiletries there, please," I tell her before hanging up.

The last thing I want is to even step foot in my bedroom if Alex is still there.

"Um, alright," Maria agrees, although a bit confused at my request.

Stepping out of the atelier, I head downstairs to the guest bedroom, my heart thundering anxiously in apprehension to face Alex at any moment. I hasten my pace, cross the hallway, and, fortunately, manage to get inside the guest bedroom without seeing him. I close the door behind me, locking it. Heaving a long sigh in relief, I look at the empty bed, still perfectly folded and it pangs my heart, realizing I'll have to spend the night here. But it's for the better.

A few spontaneous knocks on the door startle me.

"Miss, it's Maria," she says, just above a whisper. "I've got your belongings."

"Oh," I utter, turning around to unlock and open the door.

My eyes lay on Maria and she hands me the pajamas and toiletries without any questions.

"Is there anything else I can do for you, miss?" Okay, except this one.

I'm about to shake my head and tell her no, when a thought crosses my mind. "Actually, yes, you may inform my husband I won't be sleeping with him tonight."

Maria raises her eyebrows in surprise at my request but gives a quick sharp nod of the head. "Duly noted. Anything else?"

"That's all," I reply. "Thank you, Maria."

I close and lock the door again, before heading to the ensuite bathroom to get myself ready for bed.

I wash my face, apply some moisturizer, and then brush my teeth. Returning to the bedroom, I take off my clothes and switch into my comfy pajamas.

Knock! Knock! Knock!

"Petra," Alex calls from behind the closed door, his tone irritated and impatient. He knocks the door and twists the handle a few more times, before saying, "Can you stop your stupid tantrum and come upstairs to our bedroom, please?"

"No!" I shout, hoping he can hear me. "I'm sleeping here tonight. Deal with it." Then I open the sheets and slide right into the bed.

"You do realize Maria has a spare key, right?" *Oh shit!* "I can ask her to open this door at any time," he informs, most likely to scare me, but when I don't answer, he twists the handle once more. "Petra, please open the damn door and let's talk."

An exasperated breath rolls off my lungs, my head on the pillow. I look at the ceiling as I ponder whether or not to just ignore him.

"Petra—"

"Then go ahead and ask her, because I'm not opening it!" My tone is loud and tired of his insistence. Why can't he just leave me alone for fuck's sake!

To my surprise, he doesn't answer but I can hear his footsteps finally storming away.

Good.

I turn off the light, and shifting position, I try to find the most comfortable one to fall asleep.

The bedroom is quiet enough for me to shut my eyes, and after a few seconds, I feel relaxed enough to doze off.

Unfortunately, a sudden squeak on the door cracks my eyes open. I sit immediately against the headboard and turn the light on again. My eyes are on the door and I realize Alex is behind it, unlocking the damn thing.

"I can't believe you really asked her!" I snap once he opens it wide and my eyes lay on his tall figure. "I want to be left alone!"

He leans against the doorway, his face mildly amused at my outrage.

"You do understand that I'm doing it for my nephew, right?" he asks out of the blue.

I furrow my brows, his sudden question leaving me confused. Oh! He's still talking about Sebastian's party?

"I don't think so," I refute back, my voice not too loud so not to wake up the kids. "You are using him to guilt-trip me to go. That's what you are trying to do."

Alex shakes his head in denial, his hands hanging on his pockets, but I proceed, "And you know what? How can I be a hundred percent sure this isn't an excuse you set up with your sister and Sebastian to force me to go?"

"Wait." He stands tall in front of me, looking me straight in the eye. "You really think I'd go and lie to you about the mental state of my nephew so that we could attend a freaking party?" The shock in his voice seems genuine, but who knows for sure?

"Why are you acting so surprised?" I say, not even blinking as we keep staring at each other. "It's not like you've never lied to me before, now is it?"

He exhales loudly in return, his gaze dropping to the floor for a moment. As I keep observing him, I've got the impression I went too far and my words seem to have really wounded him. I'm about to say something else, but his eyes return to meet mine and he takes over. "You know what?" he asks, rubbing a hand tiredly on his nape. "You were right, it's better you sleep here tonight."

His words hit me like a hammer, causing a pang to my heart, and now that he's turning his back on me and walking out of the bedroom, I realize that he came here to build a bridge between us, but I was just too focused on burning it to even care.

* * *

"Morning," I say to Maria as I reach the dining room where she's serving breakfast. I notice Alex is already sitting in his usual chair, feeding Jasmine and Jasper who seem to have been awake a long time ago, all dressed up for the day. He doesn't even pause when he sees me arriving. His attention remains entirely on the twins as they open their little mouths to receive a spoonful of oatmeal.

"Morning, ma'am," Maria answers, once she passes me to return to the kitchen.

Alone with Alex and the kids, a tense silence fills the space between us, letting only my footsteps be heard as I walk toward the table.

I sit in front of him, my attention shifting to the twins, who welcome me with giddy smiles and babble noises. I place a kiss on their lavender-scented heads, greeting them just as warmly.

I take the spoon lying in Jasper's bowl and continue to feed him while Alex is doing the same for Jasmine, who's sitting closer to him.

When we were childfree, there wasn't anything to distract us at the table, so at the end, we kind of had to face our issues whether we wanted to or not. Things have changed, though, and now we just go through the motion of feeding our kids and playing with them while avoiding talking to each other.

Maria reenters the room and puts a plate filled with an avocado toast and omelet in front of me, along with a green juice.

I take a quick sip of my drink, wondering if Alex will once and for all look at me and say something.

But he doesn't.

His silence is worse than the fight we had yesterday. Damn it, can't he understand how hurt I am that he wants me to go to and interact with the family involved with the killing of my mom? I know Andries has got nothing to do with it, but his mental state is none of my business either.

After finishing his own breakfast, Alex stands up, leans in just enough to press a kiss on the head of Jasmine and Jasper, while ignoring me completely in the process. He then leaves the table like I'm not even here and walks out of the dining room.

I'm about to start eating, when I hear him calling me from the doorway. "Petra?"

I turn immediately. "Yes?"

His expression doesn't hide the sadness in his eyes, and I wonder if he spent the night thinking about our fight.

"I wasn't lying about Andries," he states firmly, his tone even. "As a matter of fact, before I knew what was going on with him, I had declined the invitation."

I try to think of an answer, but my attention returns immediately to Jasper who's trying to grab a lock of my hair.

"Jas, no!" I tell him, giving his hand a little kiss before I pull it away.

"Well, I should get going. Have a good day," he says before walking out of the condo.

I heave a long sigh, his words still haunting me as I proceed with my own breakfast. Despite his explanation, I realize he didn't apologize for accepting Sebastian's invitation without consulting me first. And that is something I simply can't let go.

Mr. Jasper keeps looking at me with his big blue eyes, and I know at this point if I don't give him another spoon of oatmeal, it's my hair that is going to end up in his mouth.

"Good morning, Petra," Lily greets as she walks in, ready to take care of Jasmine. "I'm sorry for the delay, but your husband wanted to feed them by himself."

"Oh, that's okay," I answer, before forking a bite of my omelette.

All of a sudden, my phone pings with a new message. I want to believe it's my husband sending me a written apology, but after checking my phone, I realize it's a photo of

Shi taken by Emma at a restaurant, making a wacky face as she holds a sushi between her chopsticks:

It might be the sake speaking, but... isn't she so damn beautiful?

Emma has been so wrapped up in Shiori and Tokyo that we haven't had time to speak that much, but this message is enough to melt my heart entirely.

Not the sake! She really is beautiful inside and out. Take good care of her, I text back.

As I come to think of it, this is the kind of lighthearted, humorous exchange Emma and I would have never had while she was with Yara. When Yara was with Emma, there was passion between them, sure, but also this heavy black cloud of seriousness and negativity that weighed my best friend down. Now, though, she seemed free of it.

A new message pops up in the chat:

I think I'm in love...

I snort at her admission, and text her right back:

I think so too.

CHAPTER 7

Manhattan, February 11, 2022
Petra

The rest of the week is going about as I'd expected it to, with a lot of silent treatments and strangely tense dinners between my husband and I, but there's also a weird tiredness in my life that seems to permeate everything that I do. Tiredness or dullness? I can't quite tell which. Maybe I've finally reached my limit of nonsense.

Another strange thing about our fight is that I keep catching Alex looking at me with this soft, almost hurt expression. To be fair, we aren't completely ignoring each other. We live together and have twin babies, after all. It just isn't convenient to not speak ever.

But his longing glances are really putting a damper on my ability to stay mad at him.

My husband's remorse must have reached a fever pitch this morning. As I'm in my office at the gallery, reading through pitches from some local artists and the paintings they'd like to have exposed at the gallery, I'm interrupted by a knock at my door.

"Come in," I say, not even bothering to look up from my paperwork.

Mason opens the door slower than usual. The first thing I notice is a suspiciously large smile on his face, followed by the ridiculously enormous bouquet of white and red roses in his arms.

"You've got a delivery!" he chirps, plonking the vase down on my desk with so much exuberance that some of the water sloshes over the side. There's an unopened envelope among the blooms, which I gingerly pluck out.

I get ready to open the envelope, but notice my assistant is still hovering. "What do you need, Mason?"

"Oh, I'm just leaving," he says, but his walk to the door is much slower than necessary, and he keeps glancing back at the note in my hands.

"You're just being nosy. Get out of here!"

He crosses his arms. "Actually, I already know what it says because your lovely husband called me this morning and I just wanted to see your reaction. But okay, okay! I'm leaving!"

That gives me pause. Why would Alex need to call my personal assistant instead of me? I dismiss the thought, slicing open the envelope with the edge of my fingernail and unfolding the card within.

I'm sorry for being an asshole. I still have to go to the Netherlands to at least see Andries, but if you really need to stay home, I understand. Let's spend the weekend together at least.

I love you - Alex
P.S. Call your dad

I carefully fold the card back up and hold it to my chest, and a knot that I didn't know was there eases up inside of me.

The funny, or maybe not so funny thing, is that I had finally decided to go to Sebastian's birthday with Alex without complaint last night. If Julia can call off Yara for good, I figured I could suck it up and go to the damn birthday party. It'd be awful for me, but it'd benefit almost everyone else in my life, including my husband and his longing for the company of his family. I guess that if I could help Andries in the process, then the brief trip would be worth my time. And sanity.

I consider the postscript, tapping my fingers on my desk as I think about calling Dad. Our last phone conversation had been disastrous, and we hadn't spoken since. Heck, he didn't even text or left any voicemail afterwards. Maybe Alex was trying to facilitate an apology. I look again at the mass of exquisite, fragrant roses and my heart melts a little. Fine… I'll make the damn call.

"Dad," I say when he immediately picks up. "Alex said to call."

"Hi, darling, thank you so much for calling," he says, sounding unusually humble. "It's so nice to hear from you again."

I roll my eyes. "Why did Alex want me to call?"

"I see the feeling is mutual," he points out in sarcasm.

"Sorry if I'm not feeling too amiable after our last chat."

"Well, about that." Dad clears his throat. "I want to keep Jasmine and Jasper for the weekend."

Huh? That's definitely not what I was expecting. "What? Why?"

"Do I need an excuse to spend time with my grandchildren?" he asks, sounding mildly offended.

"Come on, Dad. What's actually going on?"

He heaves a sigh. "Your husband has some plans he's thought up for the two of you, and I offered to keep the twins when he brought it up to me at the office. Don't let on that I said anything."

"Huh," I say out loud this time, not sure how to feel about the sudden offer. "We have Lily. We don't need you and Catherine to go out of your way if we were leaving, which, if we are, it's news to me."

"I know you do, but honestly, I'd enjoy keeping them. I think they're old enough to stay a day and a half with their grandpa, don't you agree?"

"I don't know. This is all so sudden, and really, I still don't have any idea what's going on. Can I call you back after I talk to Alex?"

"Of course, dear. Remember, though, I'm not an amateur. Me, Catherine, and Janine can handle two little munchkins."

The mention of Dad's housekeeper, who basically raised me, settles my nerves. I don't know about Catherine's baby tending skills, but Janine, I have faith in.

"Will Janine be there the whole time?" I ask, and Dad huffs.

"Figures you wouldn't trust your old man. Yes, she'll be here," he grumbles.

I smirk. "Considering you probably would have starved to death over the years without her, I think it's a fair question."

He doesn't answer, and his silence makes me even more amused.

"Alright, Dad. I'll talk to you soon."

"Bye, daughter who has no faith in me."

I set my phone on my desk, and for the first time this week, I can't wipe the grin off my face, thinking about Dad and Alex conspiring about some sort of master plan to make me less pissed off at them. I envision them both at the office the day after our fights, both moping around, and then hatching this master plan. Those two are funny.

I'm not sure if I love the idea of leaving the twins after just having left them when I went to St. Moritz, but they'd probably have a wonderful time being spoiled and loved on. I have so many fond memories of sitting on the counter while Janine baked, or tugging at her skirt asking for a snack, and a familiar warmth spreads over me. They'd be perfectly fine at Dad's. Now I just needed to decide if I was in the mood to go somewhere with Alex.

I run my fingers over the soft, silky petals of my roses, and I think that *maybe* I can be convinced.

* * *

I get home before Alex, only to find Lily placing two small cream-colored duffle bags, packed to the gills, near the door. I raise my eyebrows, looking from the bags back to our nurse. She had the decency to look like she'd been caught for a second, before dropping the act and shrugging her arms nonchalantly.

"Alex told me to pack the kids up and take the weekend off, but not to leave until he gave me the go-ahead. So don't look at me like I've done something wrong."

"So defensive!" I laugh. "I don't mind, Lily. Saves me the effort of packing their bags myself. Thank you." I was going to leave it at that, but I have a flash of inspiration to make my husband sweat just a little bit extra. "Hey, Lily? Why don't you go hide those bags in the coat closet? I want Alex to be just the smallest bit on edge."

She puts a hand on her hip, looking me up and down. "Don't you get me in trouble with the man who writes my paychecks."

I assure her I'll take all her blame, and after she stows the twins' bags, I let her leave for the weekend. The babies are having a quick snooze, and I take the opportunity to change out of my work clothes into something more comfortable—a pair of leggings and matching, skintight shirt, and braid my hair back from my face. If I'm going to travel, I might as well be comfortable.

I'm snapping a hair tie on my braid when I see Alex's silhouette approaching our bedroom door. I feel a little giddy, excited to see what Alex has planned, but nervous that the animosity between us will be too heavy to overcome and enjoy ourselves.

"Petra," he says, his voice deep and skating across my nerves. "Where are Lily and the twins?"

"The twins are napping," I say, being intentionally vague.

"Hmm…" He runs a hand through his hair. "Did you talk to Roy?"

"Yeah, I did." As much as I'm trying to tease Alex, some of my genuine anxieties about leaving the kids with my dad come through. "Do you think it's okay? Leaving them, I mean. What if Jasmine—"

Alex moves forward so quickly I can barely register it. He presses one long finger over my lips, quieting my worries. "Hush. Lily is minutes away, and Roy is over the moon about the opportunity to keep them. You remember all those things he's already bought for them? Cribs, swings, a closet full of clothes… he's been waiting for this for some time now, love. Don't stress so much."

I pull his hand away from my lips. "I don't even know what's going on, Alex."

He settles his hands on my hips. "Let's go to Bedford Hills for the weekend. We'll come back Sunday night, but I want us to get away. Alone." He tightens his hands on my curves. "I don't like this negativity between us."

I'm surprised, but in the best way. It wasn't the beach I had been hoping for, but it was just as lovely. Memories between Alex and I were so thick at Bedford Hills that it was soaked into the very brick and mortar of the place. Every step was another recollection of our blossoming love from times past, which makes it the perfect place to reconnect.

"Doesn't it feel a little like running away from our problems, though?" I ask, unable to ditch the worry.

"No, love. We are confronting them together."

I reminisce about our engagement party, and the rush of knowing that soon, Alex would be mine forever. It was a heady feeling back then, and it makes me flush even now.

"Okay." I sigh, leaning into his body until he wraps me in his arms. "Let's do it, then."

"I suppose you sent Lily home before she could pack the kids up just to be a contrarian," he grumbles into my hair.

"I have no idea what you're talking about," I giggle.

He shoots me an arched eyebrow, unconvinced. "Petra...."

"Okay, fine. They're in the coat closet. The bags, not the kids," I say, a quick chuckle rolling off my mouth at the idea of it.

"I certainly hope not." He presses a kiss on the top of my head. "Go pack for yourself then. I'll have the car ready in a few."

I pull back so I can look into his eyes. "Don't we need to drop the kids off?"

"Roy is on his way over to get them," he informs me smugly.

"Awfully sure of your success in getting me alone, weren't you?" I tease.

He pinches my chin between a thumb and forefinger, bringing our faces closer together until I can feel his warm breath when he speaks. "I know how to be convincing."

Despite his cockiness, I wrap my arms around his neck and looking him in the eye, I say, "I won't go anywhere without a proper apology first."

Alex hesitates for a moment, even frowning at the idea, but seeing how important this is for me, he finally gives in. "Fine," he huffs. "I apologize."

"For what?" I press on.

"For…" he pauses, considering me, "being rude?"

"And to have accepted Sebastian's invitation without consulting me first," I remind him just as fast.

"Okay, I'm sorry," he repeats, his piercing blue eyes locked on mine. "And as I said in the note, you don't have to come with me to the Netherlands."

My lips twist into a satisfied smile. "Thank you."

* * *

A nostalgic feeling floods through me as we arrive at Bedford Hills in the early evening. A stunning setting amid unparalleled privacy is the hallmark of this remarkable estate. Out here, the air smells cleaner, and although I've had more than enough snow in my life lately, the fat, fluffy snowflakes swirling down from the heavens only amplify the fairytale feeling of our getaway home. After all, Bedford Hills is one of the few properties that Alex owns that doesn't skew heavily toward sleek, ultra-modern décor. Instead, everything has been preserved from its original construction over a century ago—the exterior façade made of white stone while its interior is crafted from heavy, old wood, carved with intricate, scrawling designs and white marble. The whole place is classic and historical, and it feels like we are staying in a whole different country instead of a mere ninety minutes from our condo.

Entering into the hallway of the house, my heart feels giddy, and it starts bouncing with excitement as I take in the smells and sights of it all. I didn't realize how much I'd missed this place until now—especially our bedroom.

Speaking of which, I run up the stairs, trot across the hallway of the second floor, and crack the door of our bedroom open. To my greatest surprise, my body is instantly washed over by the heat coming from the bright fireplace. But it's not only the bright fireplace that makes my jaw drop —there's a whole picnic set up on the faux-fur rug with pillows spread around and a large wooden tray in the center with food, plates, glasses, and a bottle of red wine. Soft lounge music is playing in the background, creating a perfect intimate ambience.

I hear footsteps approaching from behind me and a smile spreads up to my ears, recognizing them all too well.

"Do you like it?" Alex asks, leaning slightly against the doorframe.

I step inside, taking in all the coziness of the bedroom in absolute awe. "Who did this?"

"Maria arrived a few hours ago to warm up the house and make it more… welcoming."

I remain totally astounded. There are even candles lit on both nightstands and dressers, and the floor lamps are lit just enough to give a matching warm glow.

"If you don't like it, I can—"

"Are you kidding?" My attention falls back onto Alex who seems visibly worried. "I love it!" I go back to where he is standing and wrap my arms around his neck to appease him. "Having dinner in front of a roaring fire is absolutely perfect."

"It's simple but—"

I lift his chin, his eyes meeting mine again. "It's perfect." And to get my point across, I lean in and press my lips against his in a lingering kiss.

Reassured, we walk inside. Alex shuts and locks the door behind us, while I take off my shoes, coat and everything else I consider extra.

We both sit beside each other on the fluffy rug, and while Alex is already opening the bottle of wine, I waste no time in warming up my hands against the bright fireplace.

A few instants later, he hands me a glass of wine and we raise our glass in a toast.

"To us." The warmth coming from his voice could rival the one from the fireplace.

"To us," I repeat softly.

It's such a peaceful evening, there's only the lounge music and the crackling logs in the fireplace to be heard, a perfect recipe to soothe me after a long and exhausting week.

"Why don't we live here full time?" I ask between sips of wine. "It's only an hour away from the city."

Not that I don't love Manhattan, but everything is just slower here, cozier and intimate.

"We should stay near your doctor until Jasmine is older and we know the extent of the care she is going to need," Alex answers logically. "But you've got the right idea. We should spend more time out here."

I nod, making a mental note to take more time out of our year to spend weekends here as a family. For the moment, though, it's just Alex and me, and I intend to savor every second of it.

CHAPTER 8

Bedford Hills, February 12, 2022
Petra

"Wake up..." Alex says softly, dragging his fingers down my naked body and kissing my shoulder. "It's past ten."

"Nooo–" I whine. "It's vacation."

"Which means we have things to do, wife, aside from lying in bed all day."

I shift until I can face him, tracing the line of his jaw with my hand. His stubble is rough against my palm, and with a shiver, I remember how it felt against my inner thighs last night. The lids of his eyes are heavy, and his irises a darker blue than usual, almost like sapphires.

I wrap my legs around his, arching my body as he strokes down my back. His hands freeze when I push my hips against him, but instead of rolling us over and ravishing me for the second time in twelve hours like I want, he pinches my butt instead. I yelp, and he laughs as I scoot away in annoyance.

"Later, wife. All of today belongs to us. Let's get up and have breakfast."

I curse under my breath, while Alex stands up, trying to set himself as an example. But I'm just too cozy under the sheets to do the same.

Before Alex tries to coax me some more, my iPhone starts ringing. Curious enough, I take it from the nightstand, and see it's Emma requesting a FaceTime call.

I accept it right away, my camera turns on, and my screen displays her perfect, elf-like face suffused in barely contained joy.

"Hey, you," I murmur sleepily, sitting up in bed.

"I just had to call and thank you," Emma says quickly. "I'm having the most incredible time. Shiori is… she's unlike anyone I've ever met before, Petra. She's… I…" To my shock Emma blushes. "I really like her, and I really love it here." Her vivid energy is contagious, and I can't help but mimic her smile.

"Well, I'm really glad you do," I tell her, my voice clearer. "How is Tokyo?"

"It's amazing, honestly, the food, the people…." She gushes over and over about Shiori, Tokyo, and the trip. It's strange to see Emma, who is usually blunt and pissed off, chatting like a teenager in love. I listen, nodding here and there, but mostly just letting her tell me her story. It brings me such joy just to hear her talk. "And then she brought me to a restaurant that she had privatized only for the two of us.

Like the whole place was covered with rose petals and candles. I swear it was crazy."

"Wow. And then what happened?" I ask, before my attention goes to Maria who's entering the bedroom with a tray piled high with pancakes and fresh berries. Alex instructs her to put the tray on the low table, next to the loveseat and she does so.

"Well, she asked me if I wanted to be her girlfriend," she replies, tucking a lock of hair behind her ear, a small smile playing at the corner of her lips.

I suck in a breath, taken aback by the turn of events. "Oh, and what did you say?"

"I accepted," she answers, a bit shyly. "I really need to move on from Yara and Shi has been great. She's not controlling or overbearing, she gives me space and is really cool to hang out with. I deserve someone like her, right?"

"Of course, you do, Em," I reply, my tone radiating with confidence, but then a thought hits me, and I proceed very cautiously. "So you and Yara…?"

"Yeah, it's over." While I feel victorious at her statement, I can taste the sadness in her voice as she says so. "It's really for the better, though. She was destroying me."

"Damn right she was," I tell her just as fast. From the corner of my eye, I notice Alex is already sitting on the loveseat, picking at a berry here and there, and patiently waiting for me so he can attack his pancakes. "Emma, I'm gonna have to go. But I'm so happy for you. If you ever need anything, call me, okay?"

"You too, babe." We bid farewell to each other, and after hanging up, I can't help but clap my hands excitedly.

Knowing that Emma is no longer with Yara takes such a weight off of my shoulders!

"Did Emma finally drop my sister for good?" I hear Alex asking from the loveseat, the tray of food lying next to him.

"It seems so." I leap off the bed, and trot in his direction, before sitting on his lap and draping my arms around him. "She was so happy over the phone."

His cerulean eyes are brighter than usual, and they seem to be almost gleaming as they look at me. "I heard that." His right hand goes up and starts stroking my cheek with deep affection. "Well done, wife." His voice is smooth and warm, but also laced with pride. He then brings me closer and pins a kiss on my forehead.

My heart does a little somersault in response, and I snuggle against him for a brief moment, satisfied at both my best friend to have ditched Yara for good and at my husband to have brought me here.

* * *

After breakfast, Alex has got a few phone calls to make, so I escape to the bathroom, running a hot bath to soothe my aching body. He had taken me last night harder than I'd anticipated, all the frustration of our drawn-out fight being washed away by his hands, mouth, and body against mine. I had given as good as I had got, and the scarlet love bite on his collarbone was proof.

When he comes in to get ready, I try to tempt him into the enormous marble tub with me, but he isn't having any of it. "You're just trying to jump my bones again," he jokes, stepping into the rainfall shower instead.

"You're being a party pooper. Why else are we here except to spend couple time together?" I pout.

"You'll get plenty of couple time. Just be patient."

I sink beneath the bubbles with a frown. I don't want to be patient. I want to go back to the bedroom, roll between the sheets, and spend the day exploring each other's bodies in the slow, sensual way that can only come when we're totally alone, without a single thing on the schedule.

But, as I bathe, the thoughts I've been trying to keep at bay sneak in—not only is this where we had our engagement party, or where Alex had taught me how to ride horses for the very first time when I was younger, but it also contains something else. Something I've been trying to block out of my conscious mind since we walked into the door.

My mother's grave.

The blow-up Alex and I had this week was the first in a long time where we even talked about my mom. The more I think about it, the more I believe Alex brought me to Bedford Hills in order to take me to pay a visit to her grave. Jeez! Considering it makes me break out in a cold sweat despite the heat of the water. I don't want to go; I don't want to grieve again when I've already grieved so much. It almost feels like I'm flaunting that Alex and I are still together, that we made it despite everything she had said.

Even more than that dread though... there's something in me that longs to see her grave again and leave a picture of her grandchildren, so maybe, in some way, she could see them. A knot forms in my throat so quickly that I have to choke back a sob. *Way to ruin the mood with your own uncontrollable thoughts, Petra.*

When Alex exits the shower, scrubbing his hair with a towel, I'm not even able to focus on all of his beautiful bronze skin. I'm still too deep in my melancholic thoughts. Alex looks like he's about to make a dirty quip to me, but when he gets a better look at my face, he sobers, wrapping his towel around his waist.

"What's bothering you, my love?" he asks gently.

I hesitate whether to tell him the truth or not, but decide it's best to be honest about it, so looking him in the eye, I ask, "You picked this place so we could go see Mom, didn't you?" My voice breaks on the last few words, and I have to swallow to keep my composure.

He runs a hand through his wet hair, clearly embarrassed. "Ah, Petra." He then walks toward me and squats down next to the bathtub, reaching under the water to take my hands in his. "Only if you want to. But I know she's been heavy on your mind lately."

I only nod, too overcome to speak.

"If you want to go, I preordered a bouquet, and brought along a framed picture of Jasmine and Jasper to take. If it's too much, I'll deliver them myself before we depart. Everything is up to you. Don't feel any pressure."

Despite his smooth and calm voice, I've got mixed feelings about his offer. It's easy for him to go and drop a bouquet on her grave, but for me… I shut my eyes tight for a short moment, but it's enough for memories from her and our fights to replay in my mind.

"Then why did you get me up so early if not to see her?" I force out.

"I just wanted to make sure, if you chose to go, that we had plenty of daylight." He squeezes my hands, and then brings them to his lips, kissing each of my knuckles despite the bubbles on my skin. "Do you want to go?"

I nod again, tears gathering in the corners of my eyes. Alex strokes my hair softly once and stands.

"I'm going to get dressed and get everything ready, then. Take your time," he says before leaving the bathroom and closing the door behind him.

I do take my time. Too much of it, to be honest. But by the time the water has become tepid, and I feel the first bit of chill seeping into my bones, I know I can't wait any longer. Room temperature water dripping onto the tile floor, I step out of the bathtub, dress, and go to meet my husband. My feet feel like they are made of lead, but I guess I'm stronger than I think, because I still manage to put one foot in front of the other.

* * *

Wind whips my hair around my head as I come face to face with my mother's grave for the first time in almost a year. Wow. It's been so long. Too long. The gusts blow the tears off of my cheeks as soon as they fall, and for that I am grateful.

Alex stands close behind me, and his tall frame over my shoulder is a comfort. It makes me feel braver, more secure, and not so alone. Even though he is with me, the pit inside my stomach still doesn't dissipate.

I kneel, laying the bundle of yellow roses on the frosty grass in front of Mom's white stone grave marker. I skim my fingers over the letters of her name, *Tess Hagen*, and the rock is so cold I think I might be able to feel it in the bones of my fingers.

"Hi, Mom," I say quietly. "I know it's been awhile, but I wanted to show you something."

Alex hands me the framed picture, a 5 x 7 of Jasmine and Jasper, in front of the Christmas tree in Aspen, the colored lights reflecting in their round, precious eyes and a mess of wrapping paper around them. I hold it up to the stone, as if I'm showing it to her. I feel silly, but I don't know what else to do.

"These are your grandchildren. Twins, Mom, can you believe it? This is Jasmine, and this is Jasper...."

Death might have ended her life, but not our relationship. I tell her everything, as if she was quietly listening to me. My words come unbidden, like water from a spigot, and it seems like I can't stop. I explain my high-risk pregnancy, my cesarean, the long weeks in the NICU, Jasmine's Turner syndrome and the impact it might have in her life as she grows up. I tell her about how being a grandpa had changed Dad, and how she wouldn't even recognize him. Our first Christmas as a family of four, the gallery, Emma and Matt as their godparents... I tell her it all, just like I would've if she was alive, and it feels liberating and healing at the same time. When I'm done, the catharsis is complete. I feel lighter, empty, but in a good way. Free of my grief, at least somewhat.

I stand up, my knees already feeling sore. Alex embraces me, and I silently rest my head on his shoulder, but I don't cry like I thought I would, instead, just taking comfort in his touch.

"Thank you," I breathe, "for making me come here."

I promise Mom that it won't be so long next time, and hopefully soon, I could bring my children in person. I know my mom, in all her power and strength, her stern demeanor and warm hugs, isn't here beneath the earth. She is inside me, instead. I am her legacy. Nevertheless, I feel her here like nowhere else.

With a last look back, I whisper, "Bye, Mom," and Alex and I start our trek back to the house.

* * *

It's a long enough walk back to the main house that I've gotten control over my emotions way before we make it back inside. Alex and I walk hand in hand, despite us both wearing gloves, and the silence between us is comfortable.

I decide then to tell Alex the decision that I've made. "I'm coming with you." He shoots me an arched eyebrow in confusion, so I add, "To the Netherlands."

He stops in his tracks to look at me, surprised. "Baby, are you sure?"

"Yes. No, but yes. I'll go."

"Why the change of heart?" he asks carefully.

Heaving a long sigh, I ponder his question for a moment. "I want to be by your side for this, and for some bizarre reason, you and your sister think I can help Andries. If I can actually assist, I'll try my best to support getting him out of this headspace."

Alex breathes out slowly, letting go of his tension. "He really needs your help, Petra. Sebastian said the relationship between him and his son has completely deteriorated. He never leaves his room, he never speaks to anyone—"

"Why me, though?" I ask, interrupting him. "Why are you and your sister convinced I can find him someone to love?"

We continue walking while he mulls over an answer. "Your success with Emma and Shiori speaks for itself. You did amazing, and it seemed so effortless for you."

"Effortless?" I bark a laugh. "Alex, Yara threatened me with bodily harm. It was far from effortless."

Alex considers this. "She probably didn't mean it. She's always been as mean as a snake when she loses control. You bested her, and I'm sure that enraged her."

I plant my feet and come to a stop. Alex groans but stops too.

"I have two conditions if I'm going to come and do this favor for you guys," I declare. Alex looks at me, bemused, waiting for my demands.

"First," I start. "You have to talk to Yara and keep her away from me from here on out. I never want to interact with her again. Second, we don't stay the night. We go to the party, and then we leave, but I can't stomach sleeping under Julia's roof. I'll never accept that."

"You drive a hard bargain," Alex drawls, but reaches his hand out for a handshake. With a smirk, I put my hand in his and he pumps it once, like two professionals making a business deal… that is, until he yanks me into his arms and kisses me soundly.

"Deal?" I ask against his mouth.

"Deal," he agrees.

With that handshake, every obstacle between us feels like it has dissipated, and the fight is well and truly over. My emotions had been so high today, after seeing Mom's grave especially, that I'm almost weak with relief to be back in good graces with Alex. I love him so much, and I need us to be on even ground. And frankly, I'm so proud of us for being able to communicate so much better than we had earlier in our relationship.

* * *

When the sun settles, we find ourselves in front of the roaring fire again, sharing a vegan "charcuterie" board and a bottle of blackberry wine from a local vineyard. The wine warms me from the inside out and loosens my limbs. Combined with the heat of the fire, I'm absolutely relaxed, and there's only one other thing I want tonight.

The soft, faux fur rug we are sitting on rustles as I climb into Alex's lap, threading my fingers into his hair. He grins indulgently, bracing himself with his hands flat on the rug.

"What do you want, wife?" he rumbles, letting me run my nails over his scalp and my lips over his jaw.

"Make love to me," I demand.

"Ask nicely," he says, voice getting raspier.

"Please make love to me," I beg, softly biting his lower lip. "I need you so much."

"Only because you said please." Alex chuckles, sliding my sweater over my head and unhooking my bra. I can't keep my hands off him, and I growl with frustration as I have to stop to give him space to work.

His gaze drags over me, pupils blown wide with lust. "You're so fucking beautiful," he growls, the touch of his fingertips on my bare chest causing a rush of wetness between my legs.

Alex leans me back in his lap, his hands on my shoulder blades and his mouth moving over every inch of my breasts, sucking my nipples into his mouth until I'm ready to scream. Each pull and nibble causes me to feel more and more swollen between my thighs, warmth spreading to my stomach.

Everything blurs together—his tongue, his fingers, the taste of his skin under my questing mouth. My chest heaves, blood pumping rapidly through my heart. I don't know when our clothes come the rest of the way off, or when Alex gently lays me down on the fluffy white rug, raising himself over me like some Adonis, but I know that I can't get enough of him. He's flawless, all bronzed skin, eyes the color of the sea, and when one of my hands wraps around the hard length of his shaft, he hisses between his teeth.

"Need you," I breathe. "P-please Alex, don't make me wait."

Anticipation has my stomach churning, but when he slides into me, I nearly see stars, my body welcoming him gladly, and my short nails dig into his shoulders in ecstasy as he pumps in and out. His pace is controlled, even, but I don't want controlled. I want all of him unleashed, and I tell him so with my body, meeting him thrust for thrust until he curses and gives me what I need. I moan into his mouth, running high on pleasure. My fingers tug his hair, hips undulating against him when his stubble brushes my face.

"Oh, yes," I breathe out, drunk in rapture. "Ah!"

We are perfectly matched, climbing the peak to orgasm together, murmuring words of love and worship to each other. I feel like a string, ready to snap, my body vibrating with it.

"Come for me," Alex grits out.

And I do. Oh, I do.

"Fuck!" I exclaim, my spine arching off the carpet, not even clocking the filthy words coming out of my mouth. Alex makes a triumphant noise as my inner walls spasm around him, pulling him deeper until he's coming too, praising my name.

I cup his face in my hands, still a bit shaky. "I love you. I love you," I repeat, my heart full.

His piercing blue eyes burn straight through me as we gaze at each other in silence.

His voice is exhausted, but the love shines through still. "And I love you too, beautiful wife."

CHAPTER 9

The Netherlands, February 19, 2022
Petra

"Stop messing with your hair," Catherine protests, taking my compact and closing it with an audible snap. "You're twenty, Petra, you're stunning. Stop messing around."

"Give me that back!" I hiss, yanking my compact out of her grasp.

"Ladies, please," Dad groans from the front seat of our rental SUV, which is a black Volvo XC90 with tan leather interior. Alex is in the passenger seat, while Catherine and I are seated in the back, with the twins in the last row, content in their car seats, switching between babbling and playing with their car toys and napping. I'm already regretting sharing a ride here, but Catherine had promised to coach me on the attending guests.

She looks like she could have owned the Van Den Bosch mansion on her own. She's so impeccably dressed, her short blond hair is slicked back smooth, and she sports a Khaite sleeveless dress, made of intricate draping that is such a pale gold that it seems nearly white. My own dress is quite different; a light pink, with the skirt falling under my knees, long sleeves, and a high neckline. The entire thing is crafted of filigree lace, and I had left my legs bare of any sort of hose. I'm wearing my hair down in a straight and shimmering sheet, and hardly any makeup.

That didn't stop me from obsessively checking my reflection, though. I hate to admit it, but I'm more than a little nervous to see Alex's family again.

Calm down, I command myself. *You're here for a reason. Keep it together.*

I take a deep breath and think back to what I'm trying to protect by being here. The conversation with Emma last Saturday had reinforced my decision to come to Sebastian's birthday party. Both Julia and Alex had promised to intercept Yara and make sure she leaves me alone, forever hopefully. This is my chance to evict Yara from my life, and by association, Emma's life once and for all. The sacrifice seems so worth it.

While I'm not having second thoughts as we pull up to the valet, I don't want to go in and pretend like we are one big, happy family, either. No matter, it's a little late to back out now, so with a steadying breath, I let Alex help me out of the car while Dad hands the keys to the valet, and then the men get the children's seats out of the back.

I remember coming here once for a brunch Julia had organized, and yet, as I take in my surroundings, the immensity of the estate still catches me by surprise.

The outside of the Van Den Bosch mansion is absolutely swimming with cars, and the small crew of valets are working overtime to try to keep up. As much as I'm not a fan of the family, there's no denying that their property is the epitome of old money. The house itself is exquisite, reminiscent of something out of a period drama. A long staircase leads to an entryway covered by a portico made of white stone, secured by a colonnade. The front garden is perfectly manicured, stretching out so far that we can't even see the street, and a fountain stands in the roundabout in front of the home.

Catherine and Alex are both obviously excited to see everyone, but I hang back a few steps as we approach the entrance to talk to my father, who is at least a little more subdued.

"Regretting the invitation yet?" I ask in a whisper.

"I'm compromising for Catherine," he informs me, adjusting his hold on Jasmine's carrier. "Plus, looking at this place, I'm sure they'll have some phenomenal, aged Macallan somewhere. So, you know, little victories."

I can't help but snort at his comment while Dad speeds up his pace to catch up with Catherine. He looks great, I have to admit, especially at her side. The tailored suit, with its velvet maroon blazer, makes him look ten years younger.

Alex looks incredibly handsome tonight too in a gray three-piece suit. He's skipped the tie and the first button of his white shirt has been left undone. As we get closer to the entrance, I join my husband, hooking one of my arms through his free one, so we can walk inside as a united front.

As we wait to get in, I look slightly up, noticing the Van Den Bosch family crest perched on the façade, right above the front doors.

Like the outside of the home, the inside is equally dazzling, with a domed ceiling soaring high above us in the vestibule, all the way past the other floors to the very top of the mansion. The floors are dark green marble, shined to a reflective sheen, with mosaic tile in shades of white, cream, and gold on the ceiling, mirroring the filigreed design of the landscape art outside.

Our coats are taken by a butler, and once they discover exactly who we are, the staff springs into action, escorting us directly to Julia and Sebastian. We take the babies out of their carriers, which are immediately whisked away to the nursery area.

Their ballroom connects directly to the dining room, the green marble floors transitioning to a dark cherry stained planking. It's opulent, with portraits of the family, old and new, decorating the walls along with a vast assortment of artwork, all in frames so beautiful that they rival the paintings themselves.

Speaking of beautiful things… I finally see Julia, tall and thin, with incredibly long legs bare from the knee down and her blond wavy hair perfectly complemented by her ice blue dress. Standing near her are her daughters, in dresses of the same shade, just with slightly different cuts. They look like smaller, mirrored versions of Julia and the thought of it makes me shudder.

Sebastian is there too, the man of the hour himself. It's his fifty-fifth birthday, but if someone had asked me, I'd have pegged him as forty-five. There are only light hints of gray in his brown hair, and the only real indicator of his age are the crinkles at the corner of his brown eyes when he smiles.

Sebastian sees us first, and he leaves the small group of people he's talking to mid-conversation to meet Alex half-way, walking in long strides. The two men meet with an enthusiastic handshake and shoulder pats, while Alex juggles a mildly annoyed Jasper from arm to arm.

Catherine has already bypassed me too and is hugging Julia within seconds of seeing her. I'm left standing with Dad again, and Jasmine, who is quiet for once, content to gawk at everything around her from her grandfather's arms.

Eventually, Catherine waves me over and Dad and I have to go greet Julia. My smile is brittle, but Julia seems honestly pleased to see me, and even more so to see Jasmine.

"May I hold her?" she asks. I'm appreciative enough that she didn't try to just take her, like her mom had done before, and my dad hands a slightly reluctant Jasmine to her aunt.

Unsurprisingly, Julia holds Jasmine like a seasoned professional, immediately cocking her hip out to balance the baby. She's a mother of six, after all. This isn't her first time around with an infant. The daughters, who I recall as Elise and Hanna, fawn over Jasmine as if she is the most beautiful thing they've ever seen, and slowly Jasmine warms up to the attention.

"Look how tiny she is!" Hanna gushes. "And her adorable little shoes!"

"Her eyes are so beautiful!" Elise sighs. "Such a perfect blue."

Julia strokes her niece's cheek. "What a little princess. She really enjoys the compliments, doesn't she?"

I have to agree, "She's going to be impossible when she's older, having grown up with everyone telling her how perfect she is."

"It's good for her to have a high sense of self-worth. She'll need it in a world like ours." Julia turns a bit, and I follow her gaze. Unsurprisingly, Alex, Dad, and Sebastian are in a loose circle as they talk, and Sebastian has acquired Jasper, who has a grip on his uncle's collar. "They're beautiful children, Petra. Honestly."

"Thanks," I say, a little awkwardly.

Julia cranes her head around a little more, taking in all the guests and her staff, who are setting up the long dining room table for dinner. "Before the rest of my family arrives, can I invite you to come see Andries? He's avoiding everyone, as is typical of him, but I'm hoping you can coax him out."

I sigh, but this is what I'm here for. "Of course. Alex mentioned that there is a nursery area for the children?"

Julia nods. "Yes, my Arthur and his nanny are there now. She's top notch, I promise you, and little Jasmine and Jasper are sure to enjoy themselves. May I have Elise and Hanna take them there?"

I look at the two with apprehension, which Julia quickly picks up on. "They have extensive experience with Arthur. They're more than capable of safely delivering your little bundles of joy."

"Okay," I agree, still reluctant, but I watch as Julia passes Jasmine to Elise and motions for me to follow her upstairs.

I give the twins a quick kiss goodbye, which they hardly acknowledge, being so busy with all the new things around them, before catching up with Julia.

With her smartphone in hand, we leave the dining room and everyone else behind, and her public persona fades once we have some distance, her poise dropping just a touch as we start climbing the marble stairs to head to the second floor. "I know you don't like me, Petra, and I can't blame you for our storied history, but I hope you can help my son."

Well, at least she's upfront and honest. Good.

"Alex told me Sebastian has been quite worried?" I ask.

"We all are," Julia confirms. "He's moved back in with us since their breakup, but I can count on one hand the number of times I've seen him since."

We reach the door to one of the bedrooms, which looks as innocuous as all the others. Julia knocks twice, and if there is anyone inside, they ignore her completely. With a pinched expression, she tries to open the door, but it's obviously locked. She mutters something under her breath, before she types something on her smartphone and tries calling her son a few times. But when the calls are also ignored, she becomes visibly agitated.

"I hate when he's like this," she confides, an edge of panic to her voice. "If he would at least let me know he's okay, it wouldn't be so hard."

Julia continues to knock and call and text, becoming more and more distressed as she's ignored. She wrings her hands, breaths coming fast and eyes misting over.

"Every time I worry that something terrible has happened to him... that he might have..." She chokes on the word, and in a moment of sympathy for this woman I despise, I lay a comforting hand on her bare shoulder. She's quivering beneath my touch.

A mother's love is universal, and I understand her all too well in that second. As a last resort, she takes from her pocket, a spare key. With unsteady hands, she fits the key on the door lock and turns it around a few times until we finally hear it squeaks. Jeez! I'm almost sick with nerves when Julia swings the door open.

The room is pitch black, but once my eyes adjust, I see a single lamp burning near the shape of a bed. And seated on the bed, is a very much alive, and annoyed, Andries, writing in a notebook. His scowl is thunderous when he sees his mother.

"How dare you come into my room uninvited?"

Andries pulls off a pair of large headphones, throwing them on the pillow beside him as he looks at Julia and me with narrowed eyes.

"It's almost time for dinner," Julia says. "Why aren't you dressed?"

"Because part of the agreement for me living here so you can keep me under your thumb," Andries snips, "was that I didn't have to attend any of your asinine social functions" Oh, I didn't know it was Julia's idea for him to move back home. The more you know...

"It's a dinner in your own home," Julia counters back. "Your father's birthday dinner, might I add."

"Even more reason for me not to attend," Andries says, closing his notebook.

Julia angrily flips the overhead light on and as we both take a few more steps to stand at his bedside, I finally get a good look at her son. He's the perfect blend of his mother and father, with Julia's high cheekbones and full lips and his father's powerful jaw and coppery-brown hair. He's young, my age or maybe a little younger, without a hint of facial hair on his smooth-skinned cheeks.

He has thick, full brows over his grandparent's blue eyes, except Andries' are ringed with a line of darker blue on the edge of his irises. The complete picture is one of a serious, alluringly handsome young man. I get the impression that if his attitude could be a little better, he'd have eligible bachelorettes camping on the lawn outside, waiting for the chance to speak to him.

Julia crosses her arms, glaring at her son. Any fear she had been feeling has all but vanished. "It's one dinner with your family. Get dressed, Andries."

"There are hundreds of people I have no interest in meeting," he tells her, his tone dismissive. He starts to put his headphones back on, but Julia stops him.

"You can at least say hello to Petra here. You haven't seen her since her and your Uncle Alex's wedding, and she's come all the way from New York to see us."

Andries's reluctant gaze drifts over to me, and he examines me, recollection coming to his eyes. "Yeah, I remember you. What do you want?"

"You and Petra are the same age, so I thought it might be nice to have someone you can relate to around," Julia informs him. "She's in college too. I bet you both have a ton in common."

Andries sighs unhappily, closing his eyes. "Mom, you can't expect me to just become friends with—"

Julia ignores him, making her way back out into the hallway with a wave. "You two just come down when you're ready! See you in a bit!" And she shuts the door behind her.

The awkwardness is thick in the air as Andries and I stare at each other, but eventually he waves toward a swivel chair in front of his computer desk, before his attention drifts back to his notebook. I go have a seat, adjusting my skirt.

"Sorry about this," I tell him. "But your mom is worried about you. She thinks since we're peers, you might enjoy my company a little more than some of the dinosaurs downstairs." I'm trying to joke with him, but Andries just continues to stare at me with a straight face. "So, uh… what are you writing in your notebook?"

"You don't have to pretend you care," he says, exasperated. "I don't know why Mom brought you here, but seriously, you are wasting your time."

I lean forward a little. "Your mom told me your girlfriend broke up with you," I tell him, my voice gentle, as I try to coax a reaction from him. "I know how it feels to love someone and then to have that person break up with you. It's a pain like no other."

Andries chuckles. "That's what Mom told you?" he scoffs. "Wow. Well, I'm the one who broke up with her, if you must know. But it's fantastic that she can't bother to pay attention to the details of my relationship."

"Oh, you did?" I ask, bewildered. "But why? Julia said you two were deeply in love."

"Because it's for the better," he states simply, returning to his notebook and, thoroughly focused, he continues writing. There's a lot left unsaid, I'm sure, but he isn't offering anything else up for me, so I try a new approach.

"What are you writing in there?" I ask again. "Are you an aspiring author?"

There's a few beats of silence and it feels like my question is hanging in the air.

"Sort of," he finally replies, his eyes barely leaving his notebook. "Much to the disappointment of my parents." He pauses, his gaze finally drifting up. "I'm writing about how the woman I love above life itself broke my heart." There is a note of genuine grief in his otherwise sarcastic voice. "Writing has therapeutic effects, or so I've been told."

Now we're getting somewhere. "What did she do to break your heart? It has to be something terrible if you want nothing to do with her anymore."

"Oh, she was…" He breaks eye contact, his gaze dropping to his lap as if searching for the best words to put on, and yet, it seems like he can't find any. "Whatever. I just want to write everything down, get her out of my system, and then move on. I was just a fucking idiot who believed she was the one."

"The one?" *Wow! This was really serious then.* "You're not an idiot. The heart wants what the heart wants. Don't be surprised if just writing it out isn't enough to wash her from your system, though." Andries makes a distraught noise at that, looking down at the words he had just written. "How long were you guys together?" I ask carefully.

"Like three months, but I knew she was the one since the day I met her." He lets out a self-deprecating chuckle. "You must think I'm crazy."

I smile at him gently, wanting Andries to know that I'm an ally. I understand him, and what he's going through. "Crazy? You?" I ask rhetorically. "At seven, I was already painting family portraits with your uncle and I and our two children, so I'll be the last person to judge."

Andries seems surprised, and then he bursts out laughing, and it's genuine this time. He has a lovely laugh, warm and thick like honey. "Okay, that's even weirder."

We both laugh then, and he finally seems to relax a little, realizing that I'm not there to tell him he's wrong, or be dramatic. Maybe he really does just need a friend that understands his strife.

"What's her name?" I ask once the laughter dies away.

Andries becomes serious again, but not antagonistic. "Roxanne." He rolls her name around in his mouth like something beautiful and exotic. "Roxanne Feng."

"What a unique name. Did your mom meet her?"

"Yeah, on my birthday." He makes another one of those sarcastic chuckles, now that we're back on the subject of his family. "Needless to say, Mom wasn't pleased even though she was feigning happiness the whole dinner."

"Why wasn't she pleased?" I query, a little confused. There are all kinds of reasons Julia could have found this Roxanne lacking. Maybe she was afraid she was after Andries money, or maybe she came from an alternative lifestyle Julia doesn't agree with.

"She's thirty-five. And Mom is forty-one," he tells me slowly.

"Oh." Now I understand why his mom brought me here. I have nothing to say to that, thinking of the age gap between my husband and I. Personally, I see nothing wrong with Andries' choice of lover. Thirty-five is by no means old.

"But, I mean, you and my uncle are like twenty-three years apart, right? And you seem to be doing okay." There is a thread of hope in his voice, looking for my confirmation.

"We are fine now. But it wasn't always that way. I'll be completely honest with you... it wasn't always an easy road."

"I know, but even my parents have an age gap," he points out, scoffing at the thought of it. His head falls back onto his headboard as he then grumbles, "Rules for thee, not for me."

"Yeah, it can be. Everyone older than you will always think they know better. But if you want them to respect your choices, you have to go toe to toe with them to prove you're capable. Not hide away and let them judge you." While he's ruminating over my words, I stand, smooth my dress, and looking him in the eye, I add, "Come down to dinner with us, Andries. Your uncle would love to see you."

He leans forward again and hesitates. I notice he's wearing a pair of navy sweatpants and a simple white t-shirt, but even so, he looks so put together. Andries belongs downstairs, under the crystalline lights of the ballroom chandelier and among all the people that doubt him. He just doesn't realize it yet.

"I'll wait in the hallway for you to get changed," I tell him, giving him no choice to get out of it, and before he responds, I leave quickly, clicking his door shut behind me.

I'm worried he might lock the door and go back to moping, but after a few minutes, Andries emerges.

I'm immediately envious of how short of a time it took him to get ready, but what a difference! He's slicked his tousled hair back just slightly, and changed into a pair of tailored, charcoal slacks and a black button-down shirt, his sleeves casually rolled up to expose his muscled forearms. He looks young, wealthy, and carefree. I wonder if he knows just how handsome he is, with those pouty lips and heavy brows. The girls at Columbia would be falling over themselves to talk to him if they had ever seen him.

"Let's get this over with," he grumbles, and I grab his arm, giggling as he rolls his eyes at having to escort me.

"You wouldn't want your uncle Alex to see you letting his beloved wife struggle down the stairs in her heels when his nephew could help her!" I tease, and Andries just grunts, head shaking. Grumpy boy.

The first person we encounter at the bottom of the stairs is Sebastian, who is busy mingling with a few other men. Yet, upon seeing us, he hustles over to his son with a bright, hopeful look in his eyes. "Andries!" Sebastian exclaims. "Now that's a surprise…"

Sebastian tries to give Andries some sort of affectionate pat, but he brushes past him, leaving his dad standing alone and forlorn.

Surprised at his behavior, I glare up at my nephew-in-law. "That was rude."

"It's a long story," Andries says shortly. "Don't ask."

I want to dive into the story more, curiosity burning at me, but I let it slide, not wanting to spook Andries after finally getting him down here.

As we reach the dining room, we see Alex, and he looks almost as glad as Sebastian to see Andries. This time, though, Andries accepts the handshake Alex offers, and I leave the two men to talk while I go to mingle with everyone else before dinner.

I'm swirling a glass of champagne in my hand, thoroughly looking at what I can only guess is an original Andy Warhol painting, when a shadow appears at my side. I turn, only to see Margaret there next to me, also looking at the painting.

"Well, well, well...if it isn't my matchmaking daughter-in-law," Margaret says quietly.

"*Reluctantly* matchmaking daughter-in-law," I correct. "Do you need something? Maybe to gaslight me or ruin my life a little more?"

"Oh, Petra," Margaret tuts. "I'm quite pleased with you at the moment. My Yara is here with her husband, finally having removed her head from the fog of her unfortunate affair, and no one is any the wiser. And I see my elusive grandson is interacting with real, living humans, which is better than I hoped for this evening! I should thank you."

I straighten my posture, my eyes narrowing on her. "Go ahead then. Thank me."

Eye on eye, the tension grows while she seems to consider it and then shakes her head. "No, maybe later." She turns, ready to leave my presence, when I say her name, and her attention shifts back to me.

"It was you, wasn't it?" I ask, searching for the truth in her gaze.

But Margaret doesn't even flinch and remains just as unmoved as before. "What do you mean?"

"The sex-tape," I tell her. "It was you who hired that reporter in Aspen, right?"

She raises her eyebrows, slightly flabbergasted by my question. "I have no idea what you are talking about, my dear." Her tone is serious, without a trace of sarcasm to be found.

But Margaret can pull a poker face like no one else, so there's absolutely no way to find out the truth. "Of course not," I scoff.

She doesn't even try to reassure me, on the contrary, she heaves an exasperated breath, ready to leave my presence. "Have a good evening."

I grind my teeth as the older woman floats away over the ballroom floor, but I let her go. I don't want to extend our interactions any longer than necessary.

As the cocktail-hour goes on, I see Yara and Elliot from a distance. If looks could kill, I'd be long dead. I've never gotten a more intense feeling of hate from anyone as I do now from Yara, but true to their word, every time I see her coming toward me, murder in her eyes, Julia or Sebastian intercept her for some inane question or to introduce her to another guest. I don't know if she realizes what's happening, but I take joy in watching her be thwarted over and over again.

Alex finds me right before the cocktail hour ends, and we go to the dinner table together, hand in hand. He leans down to whisper, "Yara looks like she's about to spontaneously combust."

"I wouldn't be mad if she did," I answer, suppressing a laugh.

"It'd be entertaining, I must admit," Alex replies, humor dripping from his voice. "She should behave, though."

Dinner is brilliant, of course, and the hundreds upon hundreds of plates come out without a hitch. I don't even have to mention my veganism, either; all of my dishes come out specially prepared. I look at Julia, who gives me a polite nod, looking over at her son before raising her glass to me in a private toast.

I flash her a cordial smile in return, raising my glass back, on even ground for the moment with my sister-in-law. At least she isn't plotting my untimely death, like Yara is.

Margaret is sitting close enough to Catherine and Julia to maintain a constant conversation, but they have placed Yara and Elliot at the end of the table. Far enough away that she can't speak to me even if she tried. Margaret's middle daughter, Maud, is seated with Yara and Elliot, but she seems annoyed at how distracted Yara is as she tries to make small talk.

All in all, it's a beautiful evening so far. Andries looks like he has eaten something sour, and every time his father reaches over to squeeze his mother's hand or kiss her cheek he scowls and rolls his eyes, but he answers questions when he is spoken to and doesn't bolt mid meal. I count it as a success in my book.

When the meal ends, some guests retire to the library for port and cigars, while the younger couples take straight to the dance floor when the live string quartet starts up. I assure Alex that I will be fine, and he's on cloud nine as he goes with Sebastian and Dad to the library.

While waiting for a fresh glass of champagne at the counter of the bar, another familiar face catches my eye— Alex's middle sister approaches me with a polite look on her face. Maud is not only the scientist of the family but also the most secretive sibling of the bunch. I've spoken to her maybe five times in my whole life, and yet, her contribution to my mother's death is undeniable.

"You seem to be doing well in the lion's pit tonight," Maud tells me, gesturing at the ballroom before ordering her own refill. Her tone might be polite, her smile perfectly lady-like, but I know all too well that behind the charade, she's just a heartless accomplice in my mom's murder.

"Reluctantly, but I'm making it work."

She nods knowingly. "Sometimes that's all we can do."

Drink in hand, I go to see who else I can talk to while I wait on Alex to return. My eyes land on the French glass doors leading out to a terrace at the far end of the room. As I reach them, my eyes zoom in on the figure leaning against the railing that I immediately recognize.

I open the terrace doors as quietly as I can, but Andries still hears me. He turns stiffly but relaxes when he sees it's me.

"Hey, sorry," I say, feeling a bit like an intruder as I close the door behind us, but I want to escape the presence of those people just as much as he does. "How are you doing?" My question is hanging in the air while I walk over to lean over the railing next to him.

He shrugs one shoulder. "Fine, I guess. I just don't want to be surrounded by people right now. It's suffocating."

"Yeah, it's hard to tolerate these enormous groups when you're torn up inside."

Andries turns his gaze back to the horizon and silence settles between us as we remain contemplating the landscape amid the freezing dark night.

"You are still thinking about her, huh?" My question breaks our quiet moment, but Andries doesn't seem to mind.

"It's hard not to." He sighs, his gaze drifting back to me. "The second time I met her was here on this very terrace."

My brows furrow in confusion. "Wait," I say, taken aback by his revelation. "She came here even before you were together?"

"Yep, she was the plus one of a guy that works at my dad's company." He pauses for a beat and heaves a long sigh as if what he's thinking hurts. "The first time I met her was at the University of Amsterdam. I was lost, and she showed me the way…" His voice takes on a wistful quality, and he appears entirely engrossed in the memory. "In those brief minutes we walked together, there was something between us. Something that told me I'd see her again."

His expression is soft. It's the look of a man who adored a woman. "You seem to love her quite a bit. Are you sure it's really over for good?"

"I do love her. To the point I have a hard time going through the motions of everyday life without thinking of her constantly. But I have to move on…" His voice shakes. "I just don't know how to… how to let her go."

I consider what Julia had brought me here for. She wanted me to find someone new for Andries, but I see myself in his plight so much. His grief and deep love for this Roxanne is exactly what I had felt for Alex. The hopeless romantic in me doesn't want him to move on, not when he already has a true love. "Is it unforgivable?" He frowns, so I explain further, "What she did?"

He hesitates, but nods. "She lied a lot… too much for me to just be able to let it go." Oh, she's a liar. That reminds me of someone I know.

"Maybe she did it because she was afraid to lose you?" I say, nearly repeating Alex's exact same words. "Why don't you give her a second chance? She's just human, after all. We all make mistakes."

There's a trace of a smile settling on his lips. "I thought Mom sent you here to hook me up with some other perfect woman? She's been trying to dissuade me from even thinking about her." He must be able to see the surprise on my face, because he explains, "Everyone has heard about your friend Emma and that artist Shiori."

"Of course they have," I grumble, taking a drink of my champagne. "Yeah, she brought me here to find you a partner, but I didn't know the details." I ponder my next words, because I'll have a lot of explaining to do if I convince Andries to go back to Roxanne instead of finding someone else for him. "Do you think she still loves you?"

"Oh, yeah," he answers straight away. "She's been trying to reach out nonstop." He runs a hand through his brown hair, a few strands falling back on his forehead. "I'm so damn confused. On one hand, I want to forgive her, but on the other…" He blows out a breath, stirring his rogue strands of hair. "My family is very much against me seeing her, and she works in an industry I'm fairly against, morally speaking."

Her job is keeping them apart? Now that's strange. "Can't she quit her job and do something else?"

His laugh is sarcastic and full of hurt. "I don't think so; she's a proud business owner."

"That sounds like a good thing. What kind of business?"

"I can't tell you about that," he groans. "It's just… it's just so fucking humiliating. But trust me when I say it's not a good one."

"Oh. Um, alright." A few scenarios run in my mind, but I make a conscious effort to not let my mind wander for too long. "Look, since I managed to find someone for my best friend, and God knows how high her standards are, maybe I can try and find someone else for you?"

I thought he would laugh, or dismiss my comment, but to my surprise, Andries just nods pensively, before taking a quick sip on his glass of burgundy. "I appreciate it, Petra, but I'm not interested in meeting anyone else."

"I understand. Don't tell your mother, but I promise not to force someone on you. I've been where you are," I tell him sincerely. After all, I'd have replied the same. Despite all the highs and lows of my relationship with Alex, I'd have never wanted to meet someone else.

We're quiet for a few minutes, Andries lost in thought about Roxanne, I'm sure, while I think about Alex and all that we've overcome. Finally, I stand up straight and stretch. "Well, I'm going back inside. Don't be a stranger, Andries."

"I won't." He gives me a warm smile. "Thank you for the chat."

"You're welcome," I reply, giving him a pat on his arm.

Back inside, Julia is immediately at my side, walking with me and talking. "Well? How is it going? Have you decided on anyone to introduce him to?"

I exhale slowly, stopping so I can look Julia in the eye. "You're not going to like this answer, but you should leave him alone. He needs time to heal before he will even think about seeing anyone else."

Julia stiffens. "I brought you here to find him an appropriate partner."

"I know you did, but the more you push, the more he's going to shy away and go back into hiding." She doesn't look convinced, but I continue. "He's just like I was. If you respect his healing process and don't try to control him, he will be more likely to let you in. Love him, Julia, but you have to let him be his own person."

Julia clearly wants to argue, her eyes darting to Andries' still form on the terrace. Her gaze softens as she looks at her son, love shining through. "Alright. If you're sure, we'll give him some more time." She looks back to me, unsure. "When he's ready though, will you try to help him find someone?"

I pause, wanting to cut and run, but I remember how she kept Yara away from me all night. I want that to continue, so I nod. "As long as you keep Yara at bay, I'll try my best to help Andries."

"Okay…" She sighs. "Okay. Thank you, Petra."

She walks away, as beautiful and graceful as ever. I feel a hand on my waist then, right before my husband embraces me from behind, whispering into my ear, "I requested a special song for us. May I have this dance?"

He smells like cigar smoke and his cedar-wood cologne, and I take a moment to turn and nuzzle myself into his neck. "Absolutely."

I don't know what special song he could have requested, but right as the question crosses my mind, the string quartet launches into the soaring notes of our wedding song, "The Look of Love" by Diana Krall. I'm immediately suffused by memories and love, my heart aching with it.

"Oh, you sneaky man," I say, a knot in my throat.

We float across the dance floor, moving together effortlessly. Alex brushes my hair from my shoulder as we turn, affection written all over his features.

"How is my nephew doing?" he asks as we dance. "He seemed reserved when we spoke."

"He's... well... he's lovesick. It's complicated."

"But do you think you helped him at all?" Alex asks, curious.

Everything flashes through my thoughts: mine and Alex's history, the forlorn look on Andries' face when he spoke about his Roxanne, and the burning question of what she could've done to make Andries so upset that he couldn't be with her, no matter how much love is between them. I shrug delicately, telling Alex, "I think I helped him realize how he truly feels. Maybe I helped him figure out what he wants in his heart."

Alex hums thoughtfully. "Sometimes all we need is to see what's right in front of our faces. If you gave him clarity, that may be all he needs."

As Alex twirls me around the ballroom, I take one last glance at Andries' lonesome silhouette out in the frosty night. "I hope so. I really do."

THE END

READY FOR WHAT'S NEXT?

Get the new *Van den Bosch* series now to continue the story and meet the mysterious Roxanne.

ACKNOWLEDGEMENTS

Thank you so much for following Petra & Alex's journey with me, not only through the whole *Blossom in Winter* series but into their *Happily Ever After* as well. Getting to watch them settle into married life and embrace parenthood, all while juggling between jobs, school, Margaret's demands, and the ever-present family conflicts has been such a wonderful experience for me and I can only have faith that it has been for you too. I hope you've enjoyed these four novellas and that you're ready to embark in the all-consuming story of Roxanne and Andries.

A big thank you to my editors, Haley and Susan, for having helped me along the way. And of course I'd also like to thank my beta readers and street team for their invaluable feedback.

I'm deeply humbled by all the support my first series has gathered and I hope you'll enjoy the next one just as much. Thank you!

Melanie Martins writes spicy taboo and forbidden romances, filled with unpredictable twists, morally gray characters, and controversies. Her protagonists may navigate through emotional rollercoasters, scandals, and complex inner conflicts, but she ensures that happy endings always prevail. Firmly believing in the power of love, kindness, and gratitude, these themes are often woven into her novels. When not immersed in her writing, Melanie enjoys globetrotting, spending time with her family, reading, and daydreaming.

Born in France and raised in Portugal, Melanie's extensive travels to over seventy countries serve as a rich source of inspiration, infusing her stories with diverse narratives, settings, and characters.

Discover more at melaniemartins.com.